Drop Dead Handsome

The Painted Lady Inn Mysteries

By

M. K. Scott

Chapter One

TWO MONTHS AGO, Daniel's idea of a reunion special sounded like a good idea for improving the inn's bottom line. The local winery put reunion stickers on their bottles of table red after she provided the stickers and bought three cases. Each room got a gift basket of wine, chocolate, bath salts, and a candle for a romantic getaway. The baskets rested on the foyer table. Originally, she thought leaving them in the rooms would work, but she wanted to make sure the guests each received their baskets personally. Somehow, that would make it seem more like a gift than something that normally came with the room.

Her first reunion guest was Lorena Fitzgerald, according to the list. The door opened almost on cue, jangling the delicate bell she'd attached to it for exactly that purpose. A woman with a dark asymmetrical bob and a cashmere sweater set entered, pausing on the threshold. A quick scan of the woman's conservative closed toed pumps, pencil skirt, classic pearl strand, and wrinkle free face didn't strike any memory chords. People changed with the help of hair dye, weight gain or loss, and Botox. The woman summoned up a pleasant smile as she approached Donna.

Good, a nice customer. It was about time. All she seemed to have lately was the loud talkers whom the other guests complained about. Then there were 'the late night door slammers,' which was the unfortunate result of a not so harmonious second honeymoon. Not to be overlooked was the late night snacker. Personally, he was the worst in her opinion. Surprise hit her when she opened her fridge, expecting to see all the items she'd prepared the night before for breakfast and only finding a fraction of them. The man had the nerve to ask if they were going to have more of the missing delicious cinnamon date buns. Her lips tilted up as she stifled a sign of relief as the guest approached with one single designer weekender. *Classy.* Why couldn't all her guests be similar?

"Hello. Welcome to The Painted Lady Inn. Thanks for choosing the Lady for your weekend getaway." She held the smile in place, questioning her choice of a name for her bed and breakfast. Daniel remarked it sounded like something out of a horror movie, as if it would come to life.

The woman didn't answer, but took two more steps closer, then placed her bag on the floor. "I'm glad to be here before the sun sets."

"You made it." Her cheeks were starting to ache from continually smiling. Well, that and acting like a genial innkeeper. Why couldn't she'd just be normal Donna Tollhouse?

"Yes, yes, I did." The woman glanced around the foyer that had several open doors to the front parlor, library, and dining room. Her lips pursed as her eyes flicked upward.

No dust anywhere and the floors gleamed where they weren't covered by a floral runner.

"May I have your name, please?"

The woman gave a nervous laugh, which seemed out of place.

"Lorena, Lorena Fitzgerald."

Convenient, since she was the first name on the list. Her hand gripped the heavy reunion basket and held it out to Lorena. "Compliments of the inn for your stay." The woman's French tipped manicured hand wrapped around the basket handle beside Donna's.

"Enjoy the reunion."

Lorena's eyes widened. "There's a reunion? What type?"

Donna had relinquished the basket unaware that her guest didn't merit it. Too late to take it back too, especially since the woman was now poking through it making pleasurable noises. With her luck, the couple out antiquing would hear about it and expect one too. Well, she did have a couple of cases of Reunion Red.

"Ah yes, the local high school is having a reunion. Thirty-one years."

Lorena fanned her free hand in front of her as if overcome by the thought of a reunion. "Thirty-one years. Goodness, I've only been out of school barely twenty years."

Taking a page from Detective Taber's book, she ran a hand over her face, hoping to hide her smirk. Okay, the woman looked good, but not that good. A woman in her thirties would wear something a little more playful, edgy, or even more casual. The shoes and sweater set declared her mid-forty. Once she recovered her innkeeper face, she dropped her hand.

"Of course," she responded, not knowing what she should say to such a blatant lie. "Let me show you to your room. You'll probably want to relax. There are refreshment stations on every floor, but there are also several nice restaurants nearby."

"Thanks. Maybe tomorrow. I'm just going to put my feet up tonight."

"That's a good plan, too." She murmured the words as her fingers wrapped around the key. "Your suite is a corner one that gives you a lovely front view of the neighborhood."

"Sounds wonderful. You really do have a lovely inn."

Donna grabbed the suitcase before Lorena could. "I'll carry it. You have your hands full."

The woman looked as as if she'd object, but her shoulders relaxed, and she gave a small nod.

As the inn owner, she took the lead up to the second floor. "This inn was originally built by a besotted bridegroom for his new bride. Quite a wedding present, huh?"

Maria, Daniel's wife, had penned several similar tidbits that she felt gave the inn a hospitable character. Had to be better than identifying it as the place a stranger was previously murdered.

"Impressive. I wouldn't mind such a gift."

HER SISTER-IN-LAW, MARIA, had taken the brunt of the reservations since people tended to reserve online, and she served as the webmaster.

She checked to see the guest names. One was a single rented to Terri Gentry. *No*, it couldn't be her high school nemesis. When she initially planned her B and B, it never occurred to her that people she knew and didn't particularly like would be her guests. Anonymous strangers with the occasional odd quirk were what she'd expected.

Fate had a wicked streak a foot wide sending her ambassadors from a past she'd like to forget. The front door swung open while the sunlight spotlighted the next visitor as if he were a singer ready to solo. The broad shoulders, height, and cocky saunter forced her to inhale and cross her fingers. His face remained in shadow as he walked into the foyer.

Wyn Lansing, the same male who caused her to spend her junior year acting the fool. Her father joked that Wyn must have made up his name to sound successful. At the time, she thought her father cruel, but now she wondered if it could be true. The popular senior had even taken pity on her and asked her to dance once at the winter formal.

For a brief interval, she considered herself Cinderella. Instead of the clock striking midnight, his date had returned from the bathroom ending their interlude. Not much happened after that, besides a handful of greetings in the hall, followed by a threat from his girlfriend, Terri Gentry, to disembowel her. If that wasn't bad enough, the twit started a rumor Donna had a STD.

If Donna had bothered to check the guest list before now, she would have sent Terri and Wyn an apology note, claiming to have accidentally overbooked.

"Donna, as I live and breathe, it is you." Wyn walked forward with his arms held wide as if to sweep her up like a fast combine cutting through a cornfield.

He was the one person she didn't want to remember her. Her traitorous lips tilted up as the handsome man came closer. His wavy chestnut hair hadn't changed much. The crinkles around his eyes made him even better looking. It gave him character. She and her girlfriends had given him the nickname, Drop Dead Handsome. They were certain that his classic profile and charm would be enough to cause a woman to drop into a dead faint. Of course, she didn't know anybody who had, but he certainly set many feminine hearts aflutter.

When he was almost upon her, a woman with a sullen expression and an oversized suitcase entered. "Wyn, you left me to carry the luggage."

Donna took a slight step to the right, avoiding the over friendly greeting. Did the appearance of who was obviously his wife cause her sudden action? *Of course not.* The fact was she was never that good of a friend with Wyn, despite her fantasies.

"Welcome." She smiled at the two of them. "So glad to have you here."

Wyn grinned back at her and held out a hand, which she shook, glad the moment of awkwardness had passed.

"I couldn't believe it when I saw the mention in the reunion newsletter that you were running The Painted Lady Inn. I told Jessica," he nodded in the woman's direction, "we had to stay here."

Her smile felt tight and plastic as she held it under the steamed woman's gaze. "Ah, yes, so glad you did." Donna reached for the reunion basket and swung it so forcefully that the bath salts balanced on the top toppled out and spilled across her refinished floors.

Great. Carefully, she placed the shaken basket on the floor and reached for the next one. The next person wouldn't get bath salts. *No great loss there.* "Here, let me try it again," she joked as she tucked the room key in the basket and handed it over.

Wyn took the basket from her making sure his hand brushed hers and gave her a broad wink. Oh, no, this she didn't need. Right in front of his wife, too.

"Breakfast is served between nine and ten." With any luck, her face hadn't shown any of her emotional turmoil. There had been rumors about Wyn running through women the way most people with allergies did tissues. Apparently, it was true, which explained his wife's attitude.

"Why couldn't we have stayed at the hotel?" The wife's shrill voice carried as Donna went to retrieve a broom and dustpan. Too bad they hadn't.

His low-voiced response thankfully didn't carry. At least the man could use discretion sometimes.

By the time, she had the salts swept up and the broom stowed, Terri arrived. The woman swept in with the same arrogance

Cleopatra must have shown entering Rome. A disdainful head tilt announced she'd been in grander accommodations. No mistaking the woman, she looked the same, only tighter as if her skin had shrunk, making her face all angles without any soft curves.

"Hello, Gentry, Terri, I have a reservation."

Donna repressed an urge to remark that her presence made a reservation self-evident. "Yes, you do. Welcome to The Painted Lady Inn. Here's your gift basket." She pushed the remaining basket in Terri's direction.

The woman pawed through the contents as her lips pulled down in a frown. "The bath salts that were advertised on the website ad are missing."

Before she could answer, Terri continued.

"No way I can carry it and my luggage upstairs. I guess it's too much to expect a backwater establishment like this would have an elevator?" Her sneer announced she already knew the answer.

"Here at The Painted Lady Inn, we strive for authenticity." It seemed a better answer than *no, we don't have an elevator.*

Terri raised both eyebrows as she stared down at Donna, who had picked up both the woman's suitcase and the basket. Normally, the woman wouldn't have anything on her height wise, but with her hunched over like Quasimodo, the hunchback of Notre Dame, she was at a disadvantage.

What did she have in the suitcase? Bricks? She stood, straightening her back and retaining as much dignity as possible. "You're in B2."

"Hmm. Should I assume there's no running water?"

Count to ten. She inhaled deeply. While she didn't think it was possible, the woman had grown even more malicious with age. "Excuse me?" Maybe she hadn't heard right.

"If you're trying to return to Victorian times, then they wouldn't have running water."

Ah-ha, she had her there. The more expensive Victorian mansions did have indoor plumbing. Terri had never been a stellar student, with her graduation depending on whomever she managed to coerce into doing her homework. The woman's jab stung, but Donna needed the woman's six hundred dollars. Technically, she'd already spent the money on linens. "We do have running water, cold and hot."

Perhaps Terri didn't hear the sarcasm in her voice.

"Has Wyn Lansing arrived yet? He's the one who told me about the inn."

She inhaled deeply as if she were readying herself for some deep, dark confession. "I'm only staying here because of Wyn."

Ick. Didn't need to know that. I'm sure the wife wouldn't be big on her husband playing musical bedrooms, and she looked like she could knock Femme Fatale off her skyscraper heels. "He just arrived about ten minutes ago."

"Perfect!" The woman clapped her wine-tipped talons together. "I can't wait to talk about old times."

Talking must be code for something else.

The woman minced up the stairs, humming a dated song under her breath. Yeah, easy to mince when a person wasn't carrying anything.

"Here we are." Donna pushed out the words, trying not to sound winded even though she was. She pulled the key out of her pocket and opened the door. "Here's your sitting room with daybed, table, chair, and television."

"Television? How authentic." Terri tittered as if she just made the greatest joke ever.

Too bad the room wasn't on the third floor so she could point out where she had found the dead man who haunts the Inn. Sure, he didn't really haunt the place, since she had found his killer, but he should be good for at least one haunting. What good was solving a murder if she couldn't orchestrate a ghostly appearance?

Donna moved down the slender hall and gestured to the bathroom. "Your bathroom comes equipped with a claw foot tub."

"Quaint."

The woman managed to degrade an expensive tub with one word. Donna would love to toss her out of the Inn, but she was well aware the woman would go online and write a scathing review. She gestured to the brass bed piled high with pillows. "Your bedroom."

"Oh goody, a four poster!" Terri grasped one brass finial and shook it, rattling the bed.

Don't say anything. Don't say anything. She kept up her mental chant as she exited the room and made her way down the stairs. This weekend might end up with another murder in her vicinity. Unfortunately, she'd know the killer personally.

By the time she reached the bottom floor, Maria stepped through the kitchen door. "Sorry I'm late. I stopped by the store to pick up extra snack items since you have a full inn."

Not trusting herself to speak, she pointed to the kitchen where they both headed. Inside the bright room, Donna pointed upstairs and pantomimed choking someone. "That bad, huh?" Maria unpacked individual bags of pretzels, chips, crackers, and trail mix. The sight of the packets reminded her of her original vow to only serve homemade goodies. There would be a plate of individually wrapped brownies and cookies at each snack station along with the store bought, but her image of carefully arranged goodies on a china plate died a swift death when one guest had taken the plate of cookies meant for the entire floor.

"Yes." Donna shook her head as she helped sort out the nibbles for the three different snack stations. "Fate must hate me to allow the two people I least wanted to see from my graduating class to show up here."

"Sorry." Maria finished one basket and pushed it to the side. "You could have given me a list of people you wanted to avoid to prevent murder and mayhem."

Her eyes rolled upward on her own. "Nothing that melodramatic. I'm afraid there might be some bedroom hijinks. The fact I gave up my room to accommodate more guests means I won't be here to put a stop to it."

Her sister-in-law snorted and rolled her eyes as she finished a second snack basket.

"While I want the inn to be a romantic getaway, I expected it to be more for couples married to one another, those in a long term relationship as opposed to a casual hookup station The cheap motel by the highway should serve well enough for that. It certainly would be more low profile."

"Mmm." Maria threw her a sideways glance as her lips tilted up slightly, almost a smile, but not quite, more of a smirk. "Maybe you could call up that handsome detective you're seeing and report them for being overly loud."

"We're friends, that's all. Maybe I could." She hesitated, trying to think of a reason to get Detective Mark Taber to her inn in the middle of the night without an actual crime.

"Seriously, Donna, I was joking."

"Yeah, I know." She did, but it didn't prevent her from wishing for some bizarre issue like sulfur gas that would clear her unwanted guests from the premises. Another jingle of the front door bell had her shaking her head. "Should I ask before I go out there and get another surprise?"

Maria tweaked the bowl on the basket, before answering. "It could be A. Forrester."

The slam of the front door indicated whomever it was had entered. "A huh? Just an initial. Must be a woman then. Women tend to do that for safety reasons. All right, I'll go and make nice."

"I'm almost tempted to watch."

Donna gave her sister-in-law a forbidding look before pushing on the swinging door.

"Hello, welcome to The Painted Lady Inn, where gracious accommodations reign." She'd been trying out various slogans for the inn but hadn't found the right one yet. Apparently, her guest wasn't impressed since he fussed with his suitcase tag instead of looking up. Couldn't really tell much from the top of his head, except his brown hair was thinning a little. Not too surprising considering his age.

The temptation to tap her toe tantalized her as she waited for a reaction from the man. Was he stuck? That happened sometimes, especially with older guests. Her nursing skills got used almost as much as her non-existent innkeeper skills. Donna even considered listing she was a nurse to attract the geriatric set, but then she'd have to install an elevator.

The man popped up like a jack-in-the-box, startling Donna so much she stumbled back into the wall, much to the guest's amusement.

"Aha, I got you good."

The short man rubbed his hands together, reminding her of a silent film villain. Something about him nagged at her memory.

"Donna, Donna, don't tell me you don't remember me?" He used his cupped hand to point to himself. "It's me, Arnie Forrester.

Your biggest fan."

No, no, no. Memories of random posters pasted throughout the school with cryptic messages to her. It may have been sweet if it hadn't made her a laughing stock. For that reason alone, the man served as an open sore on the high school experience.

She tried to ignore it as well as she could. Of course, it wasn't easy when Terri Gentry made a point of quoting the latest poster in English class that included one of Arnie's terrible poems in which he rhymed Donna with Hot Momma. The rest of the year she tried to ignore people who greeted her with "Hi, Hot Momma."

He could have described himself as her worst nightmare and been more honest. The only good thing about Arnie was he made the *take no prisoners* nursing school seem pleasant since he wasn't there.

"Ah, Arnie, hello. Wasn't expecting you." In her effort to be a genteel innkeeper, that was about as good as she could do. It certainly beat pointing to the door and demanding he leave.

One of the things she never considered about running a B and B was that all her old high school nemeses would choose her small inn over all the other alternatives. Perhaps she needed to glance at the updates that Maria had made to the site that made people want to stay here. However, a disclaimer that anyone who had played a significant role in her formative years would be refused reservations could be taken the wrong way.

He waggled his eyebrows and then slapped his thigh with his open hand as if she'd told the funniest joke. "Isn't it great? I really pulled one over on you by using just an A, instead of my full name. I would have thought you might have guessed because there can't be that many Forresters out there."

"Maria booked you."

The woman in question peeked out the swinging door. "Need any help?" She smiled at Arnie before catching Donna's eye.

Donna's nose crinkled since she couldn't say what she really thought. The door swung shut behind Maria, but her laughter still penetrated.

Arnie stepped closer to the console table she used for check-ins. A quick scan of the names showed that good old Arnie was in the room she had claimed for herself when she stayed there. A small hiss of annoyance escaped.

"No worries. I admit the Hispanic beauty is tasty, but I've only eyes for you." He held his hand near his mouth as if he were whispering, although he wasn't.

More laughter drifted from the kitchen. At least someone was having a good time. Well, maybe Arnie was, too. He certainly looked pleased. "You're in A1." She dangled the key in front of him.

"Of course, I was always A-1." He licked his index finger and touched his khaki covered rear. "Prime American Male."

Okay, he had her there. No comebacks for that line. Mark had suggested she should give the rooms some type of thematic names like *The Love Birds Aerie* or *Honeymoon Haven*. At the time, she was shocked the man had come up with the romantic possibilities. It would have worked better than A1, obviously.

The swinging door signaled Maria's approach. "I have your romantic celebrations basket." She placed the basket on the table.

"It's the high school memories basket," Donna clarified, not sure what they had agreed to call the baskets, but it definitely wasn't *romantic celebrations*.

Arnie pawed through the container as if looking for something risqué. He was flat out of luck. The man's fingers wrapped around the wine bottle and held it up. "Nice touch. I wouldn't mind sharing this with you."

Yeah, not the words she wanted to hear or the man she wanted to hear them from. "No need, I have over a dozen bottles of my own."

A hip bump from her sister-in-law had Donna making a slight side step, allowing her to move behind the table that separated her from her erstwhile admirer. Maria pretended to shuffle through the papers, holding one up at random. "Is there a Mrs. Forrester? Will you need two keys?"

Donna rocked up to her toes trying to peer out the slender side windows. All she could see was Herman standing on the walk, waving. She held up her hand in acknowledgment, which made Arnie turn.

"I should have known you'd be busy charming all the men in the neighborhood, no matter what their age."

The heavy-handed flattery rested uneasy on her stomach, similar to the sludge in the nurse's lounge that sometime passed for coffee. "That's me. Let's get you to your room, so you can relax before the first round of reunion activities. There's a golf scramble, the dinner cruise, and a picnic on the festival grounds. Plenty to do."

"Yep, I read the details before I signed up. Could I get one of you lovely ladies to show me to my room?" He reached for his suitcase and grabbed the basket, cradling it against his side.

Well, at least she wouldn't have to carry his luggage. Still A1 was on the ground floor, which meant no stairs. Maria stayed behind the table, showing no sign of leading the way. It was all her then. "Come on, Arnie."

The man kept pace with her, chattering about the drive down and inserting details of his business success in the world of pet butlering.

"What? You somehow get dogs into butler clothes. Better yet, have them open doors?" Arnie's amused expression announced she somehow had it wrong. "Well, what is it?"

"My teams pick up animal crap. It runs about $80 a yard. Each team does five to six yards a day. I have eight teams. That's a little over three thousand a day. The crews work six days a week. I'm making six figures just supervising. Who knew crap could be such a profitable business?"

"Ah, yes. That's amazing." If that was his best pickup line, it explained why he was still single. They'd reached the door and since his hands were full, she inserted her passkey. Her fingertips pushed the door open. The bedspread and violets on the globe lamp carried the lavender theme. A series of botanical pictures on the wall struck the right note. A floral oriental she'd found at an estate sale pulled the room together with purple and pink blossoms. The long windows allowed the late afternoon sun into the room. A wicker rocker sat near the window with a book on the cushion. That's where she'd put down her book earlier.

Arnie stepped into the room, threw his suitcase on the bed, while still cradling the basket. He slowly turned around taking in the entire room. "Not bad. Actually, it's pretty nice."

At last, someone who appreciated the effort she had put into the room. Her shoulders went back. Maybe she'd been too hard on Arnie.

"For a chick's room."

Chick's room, really? "Why do you think it's a chick's room?" She liked to think all her rooms were appropriate for any gender.

Arnie placed the basket on the drum table with the floral light. "Hmm, the ruffles, the flowers, the room smells like perfume."

Yeah, hers.

He walked over to the rocker and picked up the romance novel she'd been reading. He brandished the book. "No self-respecting man would be caught reading this drivel. Mindless nonsense."

His remark stopped her from asking for her book back. The best she could do would be to sneak back in and snatch it while cleaning. "It might do you some good to read it. Shouldn't judge something you've never taken the time to read."

Well, she'd gone and blown her excellent innkeeper behavior. "I dare you to read it."

He blinked once, and then smiled. "Challenge accepted."

Chapter Two

DONNA'S HEELS CLATTERED on the wood floor as she scurried to the kitchen. "Challenge accepted?" What did that mean? All she did was push back when he made fun of her reading choice. Of course, he hadn't known it was her book.

Forty-eight hours and everything should go back to normal. A medical emergency, such as food poisoning at a local buffet restaurant, could result in her return to work at the hospital, cutting her long weekend short. Donna's palm pushed the kitchen door open. Her sister-in-law perched on a stool reverently cupping her coffee. Maria lifted an eyebrow.

"Thanks. *Romantic Celebrations.*" She snorted, shaking her head. "I count myself lucky you didn't stick any flavored lube into the basket. Daniel is wearing off on you."

Maria's laughter came easily. She cleared her throat, making sure she had Donna's focus. "Did it occur to you that I might have a playful side, too? Why did you think Daniel and I got married?"

"Love. You're both gorgeous, which made for marvelous wedding photos. When you have kids, they'll be spectacular. I'm counting on them having your brains, though." The oversized coffee urn exerted a magnetic pull. With the day she had so far, an Irish coffee might be a better bet. She grabbed one of the stoneware mugs she kept for her personal use, filled it, and topped it off with hazelnut creamer.

"Donna, you don't really think that?"

Since she had already taken her first sip, an answer would have to wait. A quick swallow allowed her to reply. "Are you saying you're not in love with my brother?"

"No, but it didn't happen all at once. We had to have something in common, besides the possibility of making gorgeous children." Her nose wrinkled on the last word.

"I didn't hear much about you until Daniel decided he had you tied up, afraid if you met the family you might bolt."

The remark entertained her sister-in-law, who waggled her eyebrows. "Here I thought *I* landed your brother."

"He'd been notoriously hard to land. Others have tried."

Maria pressed a hand to her heart. "Don't I know it? I'll give Daniel credit for never mentioning it."

Donna flipped through the store-bought snacks. Nothing interested her. "I should make caramel pecan popcorn or curry potato crisps."

"Anything you make is great." Maria waved her hand. "You're missing what I was saying."

The recipes should be in her loose ring notebook she kept on the shelf with her other cookbooks. A pivot and a few steps carried her to the worn binder, where she kept her favorites. "Snacks, savory." She spoke to herself as she thumbed through the book.

"What you need is a man."

Her fingers stilled on the pages. Something about a man, at least she thought Maria said *man* or was it *mane*. "Pardon me?"

"You heard me. Daniel and I both thought you and your favorite detective might make a couple."

"Mark? We're just friends!" The curse of happily married people was they were always trying to match everyone else up. For a brief moment, she entertained a similar belief, but was unwilling to own up to it. "As you both well know."

"Yes, we do. That's why I thought this class reunion might give you a second chance at love. Possibly meet an old flame. What would be wrong if you had a weekend fling?"

If it were only that simple. "Thanks, sweetie. You have good intentions." She looked up from her cookbook and placed one hand on her hip, the other she held in the air. "First, we have Wyn, his wife, and his old girlfriend who is anxious to relive old times. Nope, don't see any moonlight and love poems there. I may have foolishly had a crush on Wyn briefly though."

Maria looked up from portioning out the snacks into piles for each floor. "Do tell."

"He asked me to dance. We did. Terri, his girlfriend, came out of the bathroom and saw us. The result was she tormented me through the remainder of high school. Wyn may look good on the outside, but something he may have done in high school bothers me."

"Ooh, this sounds interesting. Tell me more."

Donna tried to ignore Maria's avid expression. With her luck, Terri would walk right in on the middle of the conversation. Her finger held her place in the cookbook as she picked it up and stepped closer to her sister-in-law. "It's been a good thirty years ago, but there was a girl at my school. I can't even remember her name. New student, but totally naïve. Wyn asked her to an upcoming dance. Apparently, Terri was in on the joke, and they'd had this big and fake fight over him asking her to the dance."

"Ah," Maria cocked her head, "so how was that a big deal? Couldn't the two of them have broken up, and he asked someone else out?"

"You weren't there.

"Got a point, but she could have seen you as real competition and the other girl, not so much."

"Then there's Arnie who made my life hell in high school. Some stupid poem of his had everyone calling me *Hot Momma*."

"Oh!" Her eyebrows shot up as she covered her mouth. Although Maria whispered, the words they were still audible. "Hot Momma."

"Exactly." She dropped her hand. Despite everything, she could see the humor. "Oh, I forgot to tell you that Arnie is a Dog Crap Butler Millionaire."

"No. You can't be serious."

"I am."

Maria held her hands up. "I officially forbid you to have anything to do with the man. Imagine Thanksgiving with the Dog Crap King. Yuk!"

"Dog Crap *Butler*, but you're right. I'll get more satisfaction out of whipping up a bunch of curry chips than dating." She propped the book open. "I have plenty of potatoes."

A slight tapping sounded on the back door glass. Herman stood on the other side with a hopeful expression. At her hand motion, he opened the door. "Right on time."

He rubbed his hands together. "What yummy thing are you making?"

"Curry potato crisps." She placed the curry powder next to the sea salt and olive oil she'd already set on the counter.

"Phooey. I don't want foreign food. How about some shortening bread? The last batch you made melted in my mouth."

The chatty neighbor had wormed his way into her heart. He was the first neighbor to be friendly. Donna's eyes rolled upward as she considered the rest of her neighbors. The majority tramped through the place and gobbled down her refreshments during her open house. Most wanted to see where the murder had happened, perhaps imagining the culprit creeping up the stairs. It had to be better than the neighbors searching for the Lowery Diamonds.

Marjorie Hoffman asked if she'd consider catering her book club. Donna ducked the job by saying she was busy. If she couldn't be accepted as an equal, there'd be no way they'd get any more delicious treats.

Herman's remarks did not deter her from counting out a dozen Yukon Gold potatoes. "Shortbread originated in Scotland, one of those foreign countries."

"Not too foreign. They still speak English." Herman grabbed a cup and helped himself to the coffee. "I see what you're trying to do, Missy. You're not fooling me. Here I was ready to tell you the rest of the Lowery Diamonds story."

Maria clapped her hands together. "Tell me, I've never heard the story."

"Well." Herman pulled up a stool to face his audience of one. "More than a century ago, there were these fabulous jewels. The Lowery Diamonds."

Of course, he'd start at the beginning. Donna half-listened as she scrubbed, then cut the potatoes into thin slices. So far, Herman had never gotten past the missing diamonds and dead alleged criminals. He inferred the inn was involved somehow, but she'd never been clear about how it was involved. The man might not even remember the story. The couple of times he had told it previously, some of the characters changed places. The tale of alleged jewel thieves and murder probably served as his entry to several coffee invitations and the occasional meal. It had worked on her.

Maria asked questions, prolonging the story. Right about now,

Herman's watch alarm should go off, reminding him he had a pill to take. The man had his hand cupped over the watch, which meant he hoped to mute it.

She had even saved some shortbread for him. Thirty seconds in the microwave should do it. The bell dinged, stopping the old man in the middle of his narration. His avid expression almost made her laugh.

Instead of giving him the treat immediately, she held it up, allowing the smell to waft through the air. "I'm going to trot this off to one of our guests." Donna acted as if she would head upstairs. Herman's face fell. It almost broke her heart. Goodness, she only meant to tease the man, but she felt like she'd just kicked a puppy.

"Here." She placed the plate in front of him. "Did you seriously think I'd take your shortbread to some stranger?"

"Nope." He smirked. "Took you long enough to offer it to me."

The man played her. "You're spoiled. No one else who lived here ever fed you."

He looked almost apologetic before he added, "I could always get someone to buy me a beer when the VFW used this building by telling them I served in the War."

"Really?" Maria rested her chin on her folded hands. "Where?"

Herman's reply was somewhat muffled since he was shoving shortbread into his mouth as fast as he could. "Panama."

"Why Panama? World War II?" It wasn't what she expected to hear. She wondered if Herman had mentioned that fact to his drink buyers.

"Panama Canal. That particular piece of real estate was very important for transporting things. The belief was the Germans or even the Japanese would take control of it. Not sure if they even considered doing so, though. I spent most of my time playing cards with the locals and watching boats pass through the canal. Someone had to do it."

"You're right. Your story feels authentic, it's better than the one about Lowery Diamonds hidden in the inn."

The kitchen door swung out a bit, catching Donna's eye. Someone had been listening at the door. She angled her head in that direction. Maria slid off her stool to investigate.

Herman held up his hands in protest. "I never said the diamonds were here. No one knows where they are. Plenty of people have looked through the years. No one has turned up rich yet."

"You know more than I do." The murder that had happened on her top floor came to mind. The killer didn't mention looking for diamonds, but criminals seldom reveal their true intent. If treasure hunting was the motivation, then the killer could return about the time she finally retired from the hospital to manage the inn full time.

Herman kept talking between bites of shortbread. "I'm not saying they aren't here, considering the house was being built at the time. They could even be in the foundation."

Her eyebrows shot up at the idea of someone encasing valuable jewels in cement. "Not likely." The last thing she needed was some fortune hunter taking a jackhammer to her foundation.

"Okay, maybe not that, but someplace that wasn't easy to get to or someone would have found them already." Herman crossed his arms and nodded his head as if the matter were settled.

The slight tattoo of heels meant Maria was on her way back. The door swung open and Maria shook her head as she entered.

Nothing. All it meant was whoever was listening at the door was quick enough to move away. Had to be one of the guests. If they wanted something such as more towels or bottled water, then he or she should have at least hung around until someone popped out of the door. Arnie might hope to have another run at her with his dubious charm. It could have also been the spiteful Terri Gentry. In her high school years, she did a good business of gathering secrets and blackmailing people with them. Her demands usually consisted of homework or homecoming queen votes. Still, she wielded her power as proficiently as any tyrant.

Herman gave a sly smile as if he had won the debate. The man kept up on the neighborhood happenings. When he couldn't resurrect any good stories about Mr. Patel's wife deliberately locking her pajama-clad husband out of the house or the Dubois boy getting caught painting graffiti on the school building, he dropped back to the diamond story.

"Got to go." Herman held up one hand as he headed out the back door.

Maria and she both chorused their goodbyes as the elderly man left.

At the click of the latch catching, she caught her sister-in-law's eyes. "Well?"

"Didn't see anyone, but there was a lingering scent of perfume."

A woman. Could be Terri or Wyn's wife doing some investigative work of her own. "What type of perfume?"

Maria put a manicured hand on her hip and struck a pose. "Do I look like I work the perfume counter at Saks? The best I can tell you it was strong. Ya' know, the way old women tend to wear perfume."

It didn't sound like either woman. With no answer, she might as well finish the potato crisps. A thin coat of olive oil coated the lipped cookie sheet she was using. Purists might pan fry them, but those people were probably not running an inn in their spare time. She rinsed the chips, patted them dry, before liberally coating them with the spice mixture. "What other guests should I expect today?"

Maria held up one hand as she counted off the rooms on her fingers. "Okay, we have your old crush and his wife."

"Not my old crush. Personally, I pity his wife." She placed the coated slices onto the cookie sheet.

Maria drummed her nails on the counter before adding, "The cute antiquing couple is staying for a couple of days."

"Dean and Marvin are sweeties. I could use a few more like them."

Her remark caused Maria to chuckle. "Definitely. They went crazy over the décor, asking where you got everything. If that wasn't enough, they love your breakfast."

"Yeah, that's what I mean. Good people. Who else?" The recipe specified 400 degrees, but she twisted the oven dial to 425. That would make the crisps crispier.

"I'll need to pull up the list." The sound of fingernails hitting the keys signaled her efforts. "Okay. We have the Babbles."

"Who, or should I say, what? Are you sure you didn't just make that name up?" Now that she discovered Maria had a secret mischievous side, she never knew what to expect.

"Nope. They booked on-line, their credit card went through, which means George Babble is a legitimate name. The wife Helen called and asked about formal wear shops because they were attending a wedding."

"Hmm," she murmured to prove she was listening. The preheat buzzer dinged. Time to place her cookie sheet into the oven and hope for the best. "Did you recommend Darlene's Fancy Duds?"

"I had to. I couldn't think of anything else." Darlene's store was the only place in town to rent tuxedos. "I hope they don't mind the pastel jackets with crush velvet trim."

"She has some basic black ones, too."

"True." Donna tightened the lids on the spices before putting them back in the cabinet. "Not too many brides want to be standing next to a man who looks as if he belongs in a 1970's movie."

"Probably a horror movie that included promiscuous teens in formal wear."

"Why promiscuous?"

"Duh, Donna, they're always the ones who get killed first. The wallflower girls escape to scream another day. Didn't you watch any movies as a teen?"

She had, but not the same ones Maria had. "Some." A quick wipe of the counter cleaned away any errant spices. Hot olive oil and curry aroma wafted from the oven. "Okay, that's only six rooms filled. I had to give up my room because we needed eight rooms."

"We do." Maria glanced down at her laptop. "A Jeff D. Fergusson, who is here on business. Then there's Eunice Ledbetter. I don't know anything about her."

Before Donna could ask, a smiling elderly woman stood in the kitchen door entrance. A sporty hat with a feather adorned her head. A no-nonsense safari type dress covered her rounded torso, reminiscent of the heroines' garb in the black and white jungle adventure movies. A pair of tiny, low-heeled walking boots completed the ensemble.

"I heard my name so I decided to come in."

Maria cut her eyes to Donna's, confirming they were facing their perfumed eavesdropper.

"Hello…" She hesitated, trying to remember what name Maria said last. A quick peek at the computer helped. "…Eunice. I didn't hear the front door bell."

"That's because I came in the side door. I prefer to take a different approach to things."

The side door was unlocked? Maria shrugged, indicating she hadn't checked the door. The better question would be how long had it been unlocked or did a guest purposely unlock it.

"I see." Donna bobbed her head as if it all made sense. "Well, I guess you'll want to get to your room then."

Eunice sauntered into the kitchen, sniffed the air, and wandered about as if she owned the place. "I'm in no hurry. It's just a bed and bath."

Before Donna could respond to the comment, Eunice circled the kitchen, even opening the fridge. The woman inserting herself into the room and peeking into everything both annoyed and amused her. Grandmother Cici used to brag about how she peered into people's medicine cabinets while using the bathroom.

Maria pushed away from the counter and closed the fridge with one hand. "Guests aren't allowed use of the kitchen fridge. Board of Health Regulations."

The woman stepped back and narrowed her eyes.

Donna wasn't sure if the Board of Health forbade guests from roaming through the kitchen, but if it didn't, it should. "Yes, that's right." Jasper, her dog, who had slept through people tramping through the inn, chose that moment to raise his head from his bed in the corner of the room and give a feeble growl.

Eunice pointed to Jasper. "I can't be in here, but that creature can."

Jasper growled a little louder. Personally, Donna felt he never cared for the creature label.

"Jasper is part owner, therefore he can go wherever he wishes." She held out her arm, gesturing to the door. "Let me show you to your room."

Instead of moving, the woman held her ground by the fridge.

"I'm sorry I insulted your pet, but I don't want to go to my room. *My lonely room.*" The woman injected pathos into the last three words.

Donna wanted to ask her how she knew the room was a lonely one when she hadn't even seen it. It could be a friendly, welcoming room. She had worked hard to make the rooms cozy, adorable, even slightly quirky with whimsical bathrobes that included a quilted paisley to a faux leopard print. "You're in luck. We didn't put you in the lonely room. Maria, what room is Eunice's?"

"C4."

Donna did a double take and mouthed the room number. "C4?" Maria tilted her chin, confirming the number. *Oh great,* put the old lady on the highest floor, next to Wyn, who might be slamming doors all night. It was also the bedroom closest to where she'd found the body.

The last thing she needed was a one-star review about no elevator. As for the lack of an elevator, she got around it by designating the bedroom she used as a handicapped suite. There was a ramp to the side door, since there was no easy way to put one to the front door without making it an eyesore. She had explained to the inspector that it made a shorter distance between the parking lot and door. The inn wasn't big enough for a person to become lost. All the public rooms were on the first floor, too. "Room C4 is on the top floor. I could change the rooms around where you wouldn't have to trot up steps."

Eunice boosted herself up onto one of the tall stools surrounding the island. "Could you?"

Donna gave her a forced smile as she considered what she'd have to offer Arnie to get him to move up to the top floor. "I'll go take care of it. Maria could make you some tea."

"That sounds lovely." Eunice placed her hands in a prayer position as she spoke. "I'd love some little finger sandwiches. Haven't had a bite to eat."

"Sure." She agreed, anxious to get the room switch done. Good chance she'd have to clean the room. A prolonged tea might do the trick.

"I can't wait." Eunice's excitement fizzled as she asked with a plaintive expression, "Do you have any of those delicious looking scones or pastries featured on the website?"

The woman was determined to wiggle high tea out of her while she changed her room. "I'm sure Maria can find some for you."

Her hand was on the door when Eunice asked, "Clotted cream?"

"Yes. Perhaps you'd be more comfortable in the dining room."

She spun her stool to rest her hands on the island countertop. "No thank you, I prefer the kitchen, which is where everything happens."

Maria winked as she turned to leave. Bossy Eunice didn't annoy her sister-in-law. The elderly woman knew what she wanted and wasn't afraid to manipulate things in her favor. The attitude sounded familiar, but she just couldn't place it. What she needed to do was to appeal to Arnie's good nature. Still, she had rejected his first overture. Why should the man be nice to her now?

Chapter Three

Donna's upraised fist hesitated inches from Arnie's door. Favors were normally something she avoided. The door swung open before she could decide. Arnie greeted her with a knowing look.

"You couldn't stay away."

Remarks like that explained why the man wasn't married. "Yes, you're right, but for different reasons."

Donna aimed her eyes straight ahead but found herself staring at Arnie's shiny forehead. A downward glance revealed the man had shucked his shoes upon entering the room. He earned points for that since sock feet put less wear on her oriental rugs. Moreover, considering his business, it would be preferable if he padded around in his socks the entire stay.

Hadn't she read something recently in a psychology journal that both men and women flirt to get better service? No doubt that was what the man was doing. Maybe she could use the same technique to move him upstairs. *Never mind, she never had an inner vixen.*

Smile. Her lips tugged up in one she deemed her innkeeper smile. Her brother nicknamed it *'I'm trying not to belch'* expression. "Arnie, the silliest thing happened. You won't believe it." She giggled and tapped his arm.

His eyebrows went up, due to her heels, she had to drop her chin the tiniest bit to notice. His hands swept up in a prayer position before entwining his fingers together. "Oh really? Tell me more."

Wow, this was much harder than she realized it was going to be. *Appeal to his vanity. Where did that suggestion come from?* It might work though. All she knew was she had to get him up two flights of stairs.

"I, ah…" She hesitated, not wanting to admit to a mistake that she did not make. "…put you in the wrong room."

"I see." A cunning light appeared in his eyes. "Go on."

"You're actually on the third floor." This was bound not to please so she tried to sweeten the deal. "There's a much better view from that floor and no street noises."

She didn't need to point out there were hardly any evening ruckus since most of the residents were snug in their homes by nine at night. What else could she add? Arnie stared without comment. The principle issue would be the stairs.

Here goes nothing. "A strong, virile man like yourself would have no problems with the stairs."

His lips lifted and a slight sheen of interest enlarged his pupils. He dropped his folded hands, lifted one finger as if at an auction and discreetly bidding. "Would it be more private?"

"Absolutely." She nodded. The selling point she needed. "Very. Down here," she gestured to the room behind him, "you'd hear all the early birds and night owls roaming. You'd even hear me starting breakfast. Upstairs, you could sleep in."

"Sounds good, but if I sleep in I might miss breakfast." His nose wrinkled a little as if he found the idea amusing.

He was a negotiator. No wonder he was a successful business-man. She'd have to give him something. "I'll bring you breakfast whenever you wake up. All you have to do is call." She looked around to make sure no guests lingered in the foyer. The last thing she needed was everyone wanting breakfast delivered.

His hand stroked his chin as he contemplated the idea. He was taking too long, and she didn't have anything else to offer him. "I'll help you move." She pushed into the room, jostling him in the process. Donna grabbed his suitcase, thankfully still packed.

Arnie spun around and shot her a curious look before smirking. "A woman who takes charge. That could be fun."

He murmured the words more to himself. Just as well, she had no snappy comeback. Her current book had moved from the chair to the bed, demonstrating the man had been reading it. Surprise, Arnie had taken her advice about men reading romances. He toed on his shoes and took the suitcase from her. No fight from Donna since she was tired from trotting suitcases up the stairs.

"I'll get your gift basket." She tucked the book into the basket. The man might want to finish it, although he'd probably deny ever starting it. The basket rested on one hip as she led Arnie up the stairs. As many times as she'd been up and down the stairs today, there was no need to go to the gym. "This is a really great room I'm taking you to. One of my personal favorites. It has everything you'll need."

"Really?"

"Oh, yes." She wasn't sure what he needed. It probably wasn't a cozy bathrobe or French milled soap. "Tell me what you want."

The man coughed behind her as opposed to answering. She stopped walking, giving him time to clear his throat, and it gave her a breather. Arnie stepped up next to her, his arm brushing hers since his large suitcase narrowed the passageway.

"Almost there," she added not knowing what else to say. A door slam signaled someone was roaming on the second floor. They reached the second floor landing only to find Terri raiding the snack corner. Should have known she'd be a slammer. She nodded at the woman with no intention of speaking to her. Terri held up a hand but continued chewing her cookie. Arnie didn't speak, probably because he was using the few feet of level space to catch his breath.

At the third floor landing, she put down the basket and made a pretense of looking for the key. What she really was doing was giving Arnie time to compose himself. Stairs could be a challenge if you weren't used to walking up them, especially with a heavy bag. Maybe she needed to rethink the elevator as soon as she put away enough money.

Once Arnie's breath slowed to a normal rate, she mysteriously located her key. "Ah, here it is." She pulled the key out of her pocket.

The ornate key opened the door. "Here we are." She gestured for Arnie to enter first. He managed a weak smile.

The door next to them swung open. Wyn exited, just as Arnie spoke. "I expect you'll be delivering my breakfast in bed."

Wyn gave her an enigmatic look as he passed, assuring her he'd heard. First, she hadn't said anything about breakfast in bed, which would be a nightmare for the bed linens. Every room boasted a small table for eating. "Yes, I'll bring your breakfast up."

The suitcase dropped to the floor while Arnie gave a gusty sigh. Donna drifted to a window. "You can see the bay from here. The legend is Columbus supposedly stopped here for fresh water and provisions."

Arnie walked up behind her. "The trees tend to block the view."

True, at least when they were leafed out. "Oh no, you can still see the water if you try." Donna pointed to the tiny sliver of blue peeking through the leafy canopy. Arnie moved closer. His body heat and the smell of sweat surrounded Donna. Her shoulders hunched forward in an attempt to make herself as small as possible.

Her teeth ground together as her jaw tensed. *Personal bubble, hadn't the man heard of it?*

"Well, I'll let you relax." She turned and found herself nose to nose with Arnie. What a difference shoes made. Since she'd already blasted past him once, a second time might get a write up as a rude innkeeper. Thankfully, the man took a step back, which allowed an escape route. "This suite has a sitting room," She gestured to the overstuffed chair, love seat, and the mounted television. "It gives you a place to unwind." Almost to the door, escape was a done deal.

"No, wait." Arnie's voice carried a hint of urgency. "Aren't you going to show me around?"

Seriously, it was a two-room suite. "Okay." She motioned to the room. "This is your sitting room. You can get snacks and drinks from the lounge and bring them into your room." Her hand landed on the table indicating where she preferred the snacks eaten. They proceeded down the narrow hallway, single file. "This is your bathroom with a claw foot tub. These tubs are deeper than your usual tubs." Since most B and B's had regular fiberglass tubs, she considered the pricey tubs an asset.

"Big enough for two people?" Arnie's breath on her neck disturbed her almost as much as the question.

"Two people are against federally mandated occupancy requirements." It amazed her how easily she picked up Maria's habit of making up regulations to suit her purposes. It only took a couple of months to realize people tended to disregard rules she made, but if they thought it was a regulation they'd most likely obey it. Not sure if they thought some SWAT team would break in if they opened up the kitchen fridge in the middle of night, but it worked.

Arnie looked disappointed. "Too bad."

Donna almost pointed out he had arrived alone. That would be her old abrupt behavior, and she was trying so hard to be a gentler, more polite version of herself. Maybe he expected to meet someone at the reunion, rekindle an old romance.

Time was a-wasting. Maria could only ply Eunice with so much free food. "I bet you want to see the bedroom."

"Hmm," Arnie replied, which didn't seem to be much of a response.

Unfortunately, the king sized bed and wardrobe dwarfed the room. Cozy would be the best way to describe it. Donna walked to the wardrobe and threw open the doors. "You have plenty of blankets, pillows, even a space heater if the room isn't warm enough."

"Won't need them. I can keep a bed plenty hot."

Yeah, right, never heard that one before. "Alrighty then, I'm needed downstairs."

As she turned to leave, Arnie grabbed her hand. "When can I see you again?"

"Breakfast." The handholding told her all she needed to know. She tugged her hand back, but the man had a determined grip.

"Anytime sooner?"

There was a wine and cheese reception in the evening, but she wouldn't mention it. Arnie would probably think it was a private rendezvous. "I'm an innkeeper and have people checking in."

He let her hand go. "I understand."

Almost free, she edged toward the door, but the man followed her, which made sense if he wanted to lock the door behind her. At the door, she turned, tried for the professional smile and failed. "Enjoy your stay."

He grabbed the edge of the door as she opened it, holding it closed. "I'd enjoy it more if I could spend time with you. How about it? Maybe we could go to the reunion together?"

No thanks, she was avoiding the reunion. "Thanks, but I'm very busy because of the reunion." She pushed the door open, demonstrating her strength, and slipped out. Wyn passed her on the steps, giving her a courtesy nod. She could hear the men's voices behind her.

After a quick clean of her former suite, she entered the kitchen to find Maria and Eunice surrounded by empty plates. The woman could eat. The sooner she got her out of the kitchen the more money she'd save. "Good news, your room is ready."

Eunice stopped talking in mid-sentence. Her mouth drooped a little, not the reaction Donna expected. Maria jumped in to bridge the lengthening silence. "Eunice is an armchair sleuth. She helps the police department where she lives by taking cold cases."

The information made the women puff up like a pigeon. "Solved a few, too."

Donna's fingers drifted up to her face to see if her professional smile was in place. It wasn't. No wonder since she had just escaped the amorous Arnie, only to deal with an amateur detective. "What brings you to The Painted Lady Inn?"

"The case of the missing Lowery Diamonds, of course."

Donna pivoted so her guest wouldn't see her eye roll. "Need to check on the potato crisps." The last thing she needed was someone starting rumors about hidden diamonds.

"Donna," Maria called out, "wouldn't it be great if Eunice met Herman? He could tell her the inn's history."

Eunice clapped her hands. "Wonderful." She directed an eager look at Donna.

"I'll introduce you two the next time he comes by." *Here's hoping Herman doesn't show*. The diamonds might not even exist as anything more than a figment of the man's overactive imagination.

Maria slid off the stool and gathered the dirty dishes. "You'd like him. Besides knowing the local history, he still has a full mane of silver hair."

Eunice's eyes brightened. "Is he single?"

"Yes." Maria bobbed her head. "I bet you two will get along marvelously."

"When can I meet him?"

The day that had started out hopeful was gathering downward speed, similar to a watermelon dropped from a produce truck trundling uphill. Donna had to stop the rolling before the day exploded like that dropped watermelon. "Stay around here and Herman is bound to show up."

He'd probably pop in for the wine and cheese reception since he'd done it before. Even though Herman's stop-bys usually coincided with food, she always invited the man in. He reminded her of a deceased favorite uncle.

Eunice cocked her head and announced, "I'm ready to see my room now."

Five seconds before she couldn't get the woman out of the kitchen with a crowbar. Eunice left the kitchen chattering the entire time with Maria. Donna made a beeline to the side door and locked it. No more guests making surprise entrances from the side door. The front doorbell jingled indicating guests had arrived. Their voices carried.

"We would have been here much sooner if you actually listened to the GPS." Irritation was evident in the woman's voice.

"I can't believe you'd side with an electronic device."

Donna stood in the foyer, cringing slightly at the acerbic discourse. Angry guests did not enjoy their stay and would somehow blame the inn for their unhappiness. She darted into the kitchen and grabbed a bottle of reunion wine and two glasses. She reappeared just in time to hear the woman's pronouncement.

"This wedding is a travesty of all that's holy."

Think professional demeanor. "Welcome to the Painted Lady Inn. You must be the Babbles. I heard something about a wedding. Is it possible the two of you are renewing your vows? There's a glow about the two of you."

The man barked with laughter while his wife glowered. Hmm, different technique needed, since the compliment failed. "You'll be in room B3, which is on the second floor. It's one of our larger suites." Technically, it was a larger room, but only by two feet.

The husband acted pleased, but not overly impressed, while the wife stayed in low simmer mode. Donna pocketed their key and grabbed the bottle of wine and glasses. "Your room comes complete with a complimentary bottle of wine."

The woman sniffed, angled her nose up a little further. "Lips that touch wine will never touch mine."

Fail. Donna's forced smile vanished as she placed the wine on the foyer table. Mr. Babble reached for it and tucked it under his arm, much to his wife's disapproval. The man lugged one suitcase upstairs while keeping a determined grip on the wine. Donna attempted to pick up Mrs. Babble's case, but she jerked it away from her. "It's delicate. You might break something."

Donna wanted to point out that the woman's jerk probably just did so, but held up her hand in surrender. Besides, she had lugged enough luggage today. It never occurred to her that her dream would include packing luggage upstairs and scrubbing crud out of bathtubs.

Mr. Babble had already made it up to the second floor before

Mrs. Babble had put her foot on the first step. The woman gave Donna a measuring glance before speaking. "We're here for his sister's wedding." She gave a contemptuous sniff before continuing. "Brittani, which is what she calls herself now—used to be Barbara— is marrying a younger man."

Donna dropped her mouth open, trying for a shocked expression the woman clearly wanted.

"Exactly. That's how I felt, too. It wasn't enough that she lived with him for the past two years, but now they're getting married."

All right, the woman expected a reply. What could she say? "Small wedding?" If so, they missed having it in her special wedding parlor.

"Oh no." The woman shook her head. "It's a huge extravaganza with a horse drawn carriage, and they're releasing doves at the end. Birds, can you believe it? They'll probably poop on the guests."

The conversational ball was back in her court. What should she say? "Um, a horse-drawn carriage sounds nice."

Mrs. Babble stopped on the stairs to stare at Donna. Ah, she recognized the *are you an idiot* look. *Count to ten.*

"Carriages are for girls with Cinderella fantasies, children barely out of their teens. Brittani is forty."

Forty seemed to hold the same significance as death for the woman. Donna was willing to bet it had been awhile since caustic talker had seen that age. Even though Donna had never met Brittani, she was developing an admiration for a woman who did exactly what she wanted. Apparently, Brittani not being miserable upset her sister-in-law. If she spent any longer on the stairs, Mr. Babble would be whacking the wine bottle on the banister to get it open.

The landing showed Mr. Babble grinning, quite the change. The reason for his attitude improvement took the form of Terri, wearing a short skirt better suited for a college co-ed, flirting with him.

"George." The name came out like a whip crack, indicating the wife's anger. Terri ended the conversation and gave a saucy wave before pushing past the two of them on the stairs. As she passed Donna, Terri gave an arrogant single eyebrow lift as if to say *I still got it.*

Talk about a nightmare. She needed someone with real people skills to smooth things over. Where was her brother when she needed him? The click of canine nails announced her dog, Jasper, was on his way up the stairs. The way things were going Mrs. Babble would announce her dog phobia.

Mr. Babble regarded his wife with something less than the love in his eyes. "Helen, can you remember we're in a public place?"

Arrogant Terri, Amorous Arnie, and Nosey Eunice were all starting to look like ideal guests compared to this unhappy couple. Jasper's stout body brushed past her legs, then Helen's, to gain the landing.

Whatever insult Helen was about to land on her husband never happened. "Oh look, a puggle." She put down her suitcase and hugged Jasper. "What a darling dog."

Mr. Babble squatted and gave Jasper a head scratch. "Reminds me of our dog, Snoopy."

Okay, they weren't much for names, but they were dog lovers so that was a plus in their favor. It looked like Jasper was going to have to put in some overtime. A sudden crash downstairs didn't bode well. She handed the Babbles their key, with a fast invite to the reception, then hurried downstairs to see what fresh hell awaited her.

Chapter Four

VOICES DRIFTED UP the stairs before Donna hit the landing. Maria's she recognized. An unfamiliar masculine one was offering an apology.

"Sorry about that. My umbrella caught the vase."

The Chinese motif vase she'd bought recently was the crash she heard. *Seriously.* Her jaws clenched in frustration. If guests thought her prices were high, they'd be surprised to know she barely covered expenses. Here she thought children and pets would damage the accommodations, not the adults.

Despite the attractive coasters she had put in every room, guests ignored them, leaving water circles behind. This resulted in her putting glass on top of the bedside stands and draping the tables with tablecloths. Then there were the women who used the plush towels to wipe off their mascara. Donna stocked makeup remover wipes to save her towels.

The lovely three-foot vase that she'd stuck peacock feathers in was just another casualty. The woman at the swap meet had warned her the feathers were bad luck.

Might as well deal with it. The vase was a reproduction and hadn't been too expensive. Still, everything added up. As she turned the corner, she could see Maria and the silver-headed man.

"I'm Jeff Ferguson. I insist on paying for it."

Donna liked him already. He had to be her remaining guest, a single gentleman. Sure, he had wiped out a vase, but he was bound to be more careful if he intended to pay for all his mishaps. Her sister-in-law didn't look in her direction or she would have seen her mouthed words, *charge him.*

"Oh no, Mr. Ferguson, we won't charge you. We don't want your stay to start out on the wrong note."

Donna's eyebrows lifted with the words. Apparently, Maria not only lied to the guests about regulations, but about almost everything else. At least the man had his back to her, which gave her time to put on her genial innkeeper face. Between avoiding her high school nemesis and Arnie's unwanted attention, she may have misplaced the expression.

Donna needed her serene demeanor long enough to get the guest into his room before she explained to Maria that the Painted Lady Inn forgave nothing since it was operating in the red. Her fingers swept her face, making sure it didn't resemble a sneering monster.

"Hello," she called out, making the man turn.

Maria swept one hand in her direction. "This is Donna, the inn's owner and my sister-in-law."

The man's blue eyes twinkled, his teeth flashed in his neatly trimmed beard, as he stretched out his hand in greeting. Donna shook his hand with a firm, no-nonsense grip she'd actually practiced with Detective Taber, not too hard though. Some guests may have arthritis.

"Very nice to meet you. So sorry about your vase, which I would be happy to replace. I'm in the collectible business and could locate a similar one." He loosened his grip and dropped her hand.

Maria stood behind the man, waving her hands. Of course, she didn't want her to take the guest up on his offer. Both Daniel and

Maria thought it would be crass to bill guests for damages. Although it didn't stop any of the major hotel chains from doing so. "What type of collectibles do you sell?"

"Christmas. Anything to do with the season from embellished trees with wind up music boxes to old St. Nicholas himself." He gave a little chuckle as if the idea amused him.

Donna did a double take on the man, from his old-fashioned double-breasted suit to the holly necktie pin. The black vase-killing umbrella hung from his arm. Odd, since it wasn't raining. "There isn't much of a market for Christmas collectibles around here."

"That's what I'm here to find out."

"Good luck on your calls." She held out her hand to Maria who gave her the key.

"I won't need luck. My merchandise is the best." He picked up his suitcase and used the umbrella as an impromptu cane, picking his way across the floor to the stairs. It explained the umbrella.

The last remaining room involved a return trip to the third floor, not one she fancied. A sideways cut of her eyes took in her holiday-themed guest gripping the banister in an effort to pull himself up. For all she knew, the man could need knee replacement surgery. Too bad she'd put Eunice in her room. It looked like St. Nick might have been a better bet. After Arnie, she preferred not starting any bartering of favors for a simple room change.

"Would you like me to carry your case?" she offered.

"I'm good. It weighs nothing since the contents are magical."

Thank goodness she was looking ahead so he didn't see her expression. Had to give the man credit, he played his role well.

"I need to warn you. Your room is on the top floor."

"No problem, I've been higher before."

She expected a rooftop comment, which he didn't do. "On each floor, there are refreshment stations where you can pick up snacks and beverages at no charge."

"Milk and cookies?" he asked with a trace of amusement.

"There are cookies." She didn't offer milk since adults so seldom asked for it. "If you want milk, I could send it up."

"No problem. I was just teasing you since people comment on my resemblance to the mythical Santa Claus."

Hmm, the fact he used the word mythical reassured her. There had been enough strangeness today, without some lunatic thinking he was the jolly old man in red. Almost to the third-floor landing and the man wasn't breathing hard, which was more than Donna could say.

She turned her head slightly to talk to Mr. Ferguson, who'd stopped briefly behind her. The man had turned to observe Jasper rush up the steps. The dog's insistence on climbing stairs surprised her, especially all the way up to the third level. Instead of charging up to the landing, the dog stopped by Mr. Ferguson and looked up hopefully.

The man balanced his suitcase on the upper step and bent down to pat the dog on the head. "Well, hello, old fellow. Good to see you. Got something you want to tell me?" He bent over as Jasper pushed his nose up close to the man's ear.

What a routine. Donna shook her head not believing the lengths the man would go to preserve his persona. At least he was a dog lover. Mr. Ferguson straightened up. "Jasper wanted you to know his teeth aren't what they used to be. The rawhide bones are too tough. He'd prefer some pig ears."

She had noticed her pup hadn't touched the rawhide bone she'd recently bought him. *Wait a minute.* He had her buying into his act. "Okay, thanks for the info." What other tidbits might he give her?

Jasper kept pace with Mr. Ferguson, never darting ahead to walk with her. The man had to be a dog whisperer of some sort.

"At seven, there'll be a wine and cheese reception in the back parlor." Her watch announced it was already past four, which meant she needed to get the appetizers ready.

"Sounds wonderful. I did have a long trip."

She waited for him to tack on *all the way from the North Pole,* but he didn't. No guests came out of their rooms as she showed Mr. Ferguson into his. Before she could turn to leave, the man held up a hand, halting her.

"Everyone here isn't exactly as he or she appears."

Talk about cryptic statements. Was he referring to himself? Had to be since he hadn't met anyone else today. "See you at the reception." Jasper lingered in the room until Donna whistled. They both strolled down the staircase. Maria had removed the vase and its scraps from view. Maybe it could be glued back together. Repaired objects often had more mystique than brand new ones.

Since everyone had arrived, Donna twisted the deadbolt on the front door before heading to the kitchen. If anyone had wandered outside, then he or she could knock.

Time to make the fried ravioli, cranberry pâté bites, and mini Manchego tarts. The goat cheese logs sat chilling in the fridge with the grapes. Voices drifted from the kitchen. She hoped none of her guests were prowling in her private sanctuary. *Take a deep breath and think dream.* Self-help book authors that were always telling you to grab your dreams never went on to explain that certain dreams, like a B and B ownership, could be hard work.

Inside the kitchen, Maria had stacked the plates for the reception and counted out the flatware. Detective Mark Taber perched on a stool with an elbow balanced on the island. "Then I asked the naked man, attired only in a pair of shoes and a hat, what he was doing."

His visit was a welcome treat. With him, she knew what to expect. No cryptic messages or demands, though perhaps a bit of a struggle to pretend he'd quit smoking when she knew he hadn't.

"What did he say?" Maria asked.

Mark both looked in her direction and smiled, which meant her frayed nerves weren't showing yet.

"Hey, Donna, thought I'd drop by and see how things were going. I knew this was going to be your crazy, busy weekend."

"Glad you did." She couldn't explain why the rumpled detective's presence naturally relaxed her, but it did. Whenever he dropped in, she found herself pulling up a stool and chatting. Whatever crisis had her on edge receded into the background. The man had the same effect as a warm quilt and a cup of hot cocoa. Mark probably wouldn't find the comparison flattering. "Got some strange guests, too."

"Hmm, any felons on your reservation list?"

She shook her head. "Your mind automatically goes to crime. You can be odd and not be a criminal."

Maria held up a finger for attention. "I want you to finish the story of the naked man." She nodded to Donna. "Mark picked up a nude fellow only wearing tennis shoes. I'm eager to hear his excuse for his lack of apparel."

The detective hesitated, prolonging their wait, until Donna balled up a tea towel and threw it at him. "Okay, I'll talk." He held up his hands in surrender. "The man told me the woman never mentioned she had a boyfriend."

"Oh," Maria said, as she reached for the linen napkins.

"Wait," Donna held up one finger. "He had shoes on. If a person was running for his life he wouldn't have time to put on shoes."

"I thought that, too. Even asked him about it. The boyfriend allowed him to put on his shoes and to run for it. He didn't even have his car keys so he could at least drive away."

"What did you do?" The story sounded off to her. She couldn't decide if the man was a midnight streaker or a tricked lover.

"Gave him the sweats I had in my trunk. Then I drove him back to the location of his car. His folded clothes, phone, and keys sat on the hood of his vehicle."

Donna interjected, "No arrests? The man was guilty of indecent exposure. The other man threatened him with a weapon."

"I bet the citizens are glad you're not the law. It was a judgement call. The man babbled all the way there about how foolish he was to believe a woman like her was interested in him. It was a setup to make the boyfriend jealous. Since the man's clothes, phone, wallet, and car keys were all there, he didn't want to press charges. If the two were scam artists, they could have taken off in his car on a buying spree using his credit cards."

"They could have made copies of his cards."

"True. I told him as much and advised him to cancel every one of them. I have a feeling he will. What's up with your guests?"

"I'll have to talk and cook. You don't mind?"

Mark gave a hoarse chuckle. "Only if I get samples."

"Count on it." She pulled out the mini muffin tins and the phyllo dough she used to shape the tart shells. "Who would you least like to see from your high school days?"

"Hmm," Mark murmured as he ran a hand over his face. Before he could answer, Maria spoke up.

"I know. The snotty rich girl who thought it was funny to say 'Hola' and 'INS' whenever I was around. If she took the time to actually talk to me she'd discover I was an American citizen just like she was."

Donna's thumbs sank into the dough as she kneaded it to soften it up. "My mean girl was Terri, not sure if she was rich, but she certainly thought she was better than me. Apparently, she still does." Her fingers pinched off a ball of dough and pressed it into the Teflon muffin cup.

Mark finally decided to speak. "Yeah, I could see how that would annoy you." He raised his bushy eyebrows as if expecting a response.

Her fist punched the dough pretending it was Terri. "Quite frankly, she's only at my inn," she lowered her voice and glanced toward the interior door before speaking, "to hook up with her old boyfriend, who happens to be married."

"Did she say this?" the man had the nerve to ask, donning his detective cap.

Two more balls went into the muffin pan and under her poking fingers became tart shapes. "People don't come out and say that unless they're on a soap opera." Donna glanced over her shoulder to see what Mark made of the information.

His lips twisted to one side, the way they did when he mulled over something. "They could just be good friends."

Donna and Maria spoke in unison. "Please."

Maria held up a finger for attention. "No way Daniel would ever go someplace to meet an old *girl*friend. This man checked in with his wife. I'm expecting serious fireworks."

Donna sighed as she slid the finished pan of tarts into the oven to firm a little before stuffing. Her sister-in-law's words mirrored her own thoughts. Perhaps she shouldn't leave to go home tonight. Bunking in the kitchen, however, didn't sound like a possible option. What she needed to do was plant herself on the steps between the second and third floor with a bucket of ice water to throw on the first person who decided to make a midnight stroll. With her luck, it would be Santa's double that she emptied her bucket on. That would earn her a place on the naughty list.

Mark cleared his throat as Donna swung open the fridge to retrieve the goat cheese logs to warm. At room temperature, the flavor assumed a vibrancy missing in chilled cheese. The good detective had something to say. She used to think his throat clearing was due to smoking before she realized it was an idiosyncrasy. It was his way of gathering an audience before speaking.

"Domestic calls result in more first responders shot. People tend to act irrationally. What's your take, Donna?"

Ah, he asked her opinion. About time he took her seriously. "That's what I heard, which brings me to the unfolding soap opera here. It's obvious to me that one guest expects to hook up with her old high school boyfriend. While the man in question acts like he'd be anxious to hook up with anything female. The wife is a bit of a grump, but why not if she knows what's going on?"

Maria fake coughed. Before anyone could ask her what she wanted, she jumped in. "Don't forget Arnie, who definitely wants Donna."

Really, her sister-in-law had to go there. Maybe Daniel was rubbing off on her. Mark sat up a little straighter and directed his attention to Donna, who had filled the tart shells that were now ready for the oven again. "Who's Arnie?"

One hand opened the oven while the other slid the muffin pan in. If she didn't know better, she would have thought she heard jealousy in the man's voice. *Ridiculous.* "Please, he's someone from high school that added even more torment to an already painful experience."

"Huh?" Mark shook his head, then glanced back at Maria for clarification.

"What Donna is trying to say is the man wrote these horrible love poems that rhymed her name with *Hot Momma*, so everyone at school called her that. If you can't guess, she wasn't fond of that nickname, especially when people snickered when they said it."

"Maria!" She called out what she thought was a warning as she thumped the cast iron skillet on the counter. "Do you have the sweet platters set up yet?"

The sound of the fridge opening and the clatter of dishes signaled her sister-in-law was back on task, which might leave her less time to gossip.

Maria's muffled voice came from inside the fridge making it hard to understand her. Wha…ya…much."

Mark, who sat closer, translated. "She wants to know which desserts to put out."

"Let's use the mini-cheesecakes, always a crowd pleaser." Donna loudly continued her instructions. "The blondie brownies, miniature key lime pies, strawberry-kiwi tartlets, and the molten lava cakes, which will have to be heated before serving."

Maria backed out of the fridge with a series of plastic containers balanced on top of one another. Mark stood, reached for half of them and carried them to the counter. "I'd be glad to help out with the reception. Give you a read on the guests."

The idea made her laugh. "Please, I went to high school with most of these people. Trust me; they haven't changed, except there's more mileage on them." She turned around to witness Mark's disappointed expression. He wanted to come, but wouldn't ask. Men complained that women were hard to understand. Her initial reaction was to invite him. It would make sense, but she was tired of this strange one step forward, two steps back dance they have. He needed to make a definite effort.

The opened dessert containers surrounded the crystal platter Maria had placed paper doilies on. "How many of each?"

"Sixteen."

Her sister-in-law wove the treats into a colorful pattern, humming as she worked. Maria stopped for a second and tapped Mark. "I have an idea," she sotto whispered.

It was enough for Donna to step away from the heating oil in the skillet to hear what machinations might be happening behind her very back.

Mark leaned toward Maria to listen. "You should come as Donna's date to cool off Arnie. He's hot and heavy after her."

Seriously. She returned to her hot skillet to cover her snort. If it calmed Arnie down, then she was all for it. After all, she couldn't spend the weekend hiding out in the kitchen or the linen closet or whatever was handiest when the man popped out of his room.

"How about it?" Maria asked.

Mark blustered a little. "I guess I could. I'm not working tonight."

Please, I'm overwhelmed by his enthusiasm. Donna listened to see what else he would say. She huffed and grimaced knowing neither person would see it with her back turned.

"I haven't been invited. I just can't show up without an invite."

When did that stop him from dropping by before? "You're invited, okay?"

"Thanks." Mark flashed her a grin. "What can I do to help?"

There really wasn't anything. The man wasn't a cook or knew

where she kept the tableware. Still, he'd want to contribute. "Since, it is a wine and cheese reception, we'll need some white wine chilled. Go to the basement and get me four bottles of Chardonnay, any brand. I need two bottles of the Australian Moscato, easy to recognize because it has a kangaroo on it. Two more bottles of Riesling, we only have one kind. I have a couple bottles of Sauvignon Blanc already upstairs."

He strode to the basement stairs as if on a mission and stood at the open doorway. "Do you think that will be enough?"

"It will be plenty. Any more than two and a half drinks per person, not only will some of them be staggering, I won't be making a profit. Even buying cases of wine doesn't decrease the price much."

Maria nodded at the departing man, watching him disappear downstairs. "Don't pretend you don't know he's sweet on you. He just moves slowly."

There she goes again with the matchmaking. At one time, Donna may have thought the same, but now she wasn't too sure. She'd even played with the idea of romance and getting back into the dating game before abandoning the idea. "Un-huh, I've seen glaciers move faster. We probably need to have tea, iced and hot. Possibly lemonade too, along with ice water. I don't want to stretch out the reception to a meal, but on the other hand, I don't want any review that mention non-alcoholic drinks were not provided."

"Why don't you offer them soft drinks?"

Donna rubbed her thumb and forefinger together. Everything she did at the inn cost money. One thing always led to another. Even though she stocked water and soft drinks in the snack pantries on each level, she had people requesting Fine and Tasmanian Rain bottled water that on sale ran about five dollars a bottle. Even though she wanted the inn to have a welcoming, cozy atmosphere, she never realized how expensive welcoming could be. No wonder most B and Bs charged at least two hundred per night.

"Are you feeling the magic yet?" Maria finished arranging the tray and covered it to go back into the fridge.

Was this a trick question? Did it refer to her matchmaking efforts? If she barely had time off for a romance as a supervising nurse, the addition of running an inn didn't help. "What magic?"

"Come on, you know." Her sister-in-law closed the fridge door and put one hand on her hip. "You're living your dream."

Ah, she was. Sometimes she forgot that as she spent so much of her time zipping along at ninety miles an hour to get things done. The question bore reflection. "Sometimes, I do."

A serenity settled over her, mending her frayed nerves, causing her to close her eyes for a few seconds as she drifted. *How many people actually got to live out their dreams?* It made her remember what was good about the inn.

"Especially when I'm chatting with guests like Dean and Marvin. Other times, when I'm making up a room for an unknown guest. When all the food is on the buffet and it looks scrumptious is another dream moment. Unfortunately, I keep getting these people who mess up stuff."

"Every hotel gets some of them. They haven't picked you out to annoy."

"I wonder. Do you think the Holiday Inn has any midnight snackers wandering into their kitchens?"

Maria wrinkled her nose. "They had to have at least once, or they wouldn't have locking refrigerators and storage units."

Before she could catalog any of the other strange guests she'd had, Maria joined her at the stove and took the tongs she used to retrieve the fried ravioli from the skillet. "Go get changed and I'll finish this. It's time to get your elegant innkeeper threads on."

Chapter Five

THE SMALL CHINA plates and crystal goblets arranged at the end of the buffet completed the reception buffet.

"Wait!" Maria exclaimed, before dashing out of the room. She entered with a camera in her hand and darted about like a crazed moth. Donna smiled at her antics, knowing everything looked good. Maria would make it appear even better on the website and in the brochures. She'd have to warn her to not to enhance it too much or people would be disappointed. The Painted Lady Inn would be like an online date who didn't live up to her picture.

Mark popped out of the kitchen with a white towel draped over his arm. "I decided I should be the wine steward since Daniel isn't here yet."

"Okay, I'm sure you've more experience dealing with drunks than my brother."

"True. I'll make sure no one exceeds three glasses."

She could hear the patter of feet coming down the stairs before she even tapped the ceremonial gong. Free wine and food tends to do that to people. Add in the fact there really wasn't much to do in town.

The Babbles were the first to show. Mr. Babble grabbed the wine glass almost before Mark had stopped pouring, knocked it back, and held it out for a refill. Mrs. Babble scolded her husband. "George, you don't need to drink like that."

Mark caught Donna's eye and made a slight head gesture toward the quarrelsome couple.

Dean and Marvin were the next down. They oohed and ahhed over the repast, making her want to clone the two and keep them as permanent guests. Perhaps the other people could pay attention and figure out how guests should act. Herman came in the front door since Maria had made a personal visit to invite him. The older man sported a turtleneck and a tweed jacket with elbow patches.

Terri slithered down the steps in a dress made for a club-hopping twenty-something with its short hem and almost missing back. She expected Wyn panting after her, but Eunice popped up behind the woman.

The armchair sleuth addressed Terri loud enough to gather everyone's attention. "Oh, mercy, I think you forgot the rest of your outfit."

Donna expected a toxic reply.

"Oh no, this is a current fashion, which explains why you might be unfamiliar with it."

The remark was surprisingly nice considering some of the former caustic darts the woman had thrown in high school.

Eunice snorted and cut around Terri to get to the buffet. Herman managed to work his way to the outspoken sleuth. At least that part of the evening was working out. As hostess, Donna moved around the room chatting with each person. Mrs. Babble informed her how she had spent most of the afternoon playing with Jasper, which explained her missing dog. If it kept her happy, Donna might have to invest in another dog.

Terri stood off in a corner glowering, no doubt due to the absence of Wyn. If this was supposed to be some amorous reconnection, it would help if the man showed. Could be good judgment or a suspicious wife prevailed. Jeff Ferguson trotted down the stairs wearing a red and green checked shirt, of course. Terri gave him a calculating glance before she drifted over to talk to the new arrival. Mark took a break from pouring and waited with Donna, looking up at the staircase for missing guests.

"I figured out who your female trouble maker is."

"Yeah, that wasn't hard."

"Where's everyone else? I expected more than a sullen, aging vamp after your descriptions."

The mild chatter and slight rattle of flatware on china didn't live up to her inflated prediction of mayhem and blood. A quiet night would be a good night. "No one is required to attend the reception. They could have gone out."

A bedroom door upstairs shut. A pair of black boots and tuxedo legs appeared on the steps. It had to be the dog crap butler since he was alone. *Ah yes*, Arnie. "Stand close to me. My would-be Romeo is heading this way."

Arnie was resplendent in a black tuxedo. Apparently, he bought his as opposed to renting one in the city. He seemed taller as he moved closer. Had to be the shoes. He grinned at Donna, probably sure she waited for him with bated breath, but surely the presence of Mark would discount that theory.

She thrust out her elbow, but only hit air. Maria caught her eye and mouthed, "Went to get more wine."

Did she mean he went to get more wine out of the fridge or the basement? If it was the latter, she needed to stop him before the mixer cut into her profit margin. The bottles needed to last out the month.

A hand landed on her arm, drifted down to her hand and lifted it. Arnie kissed her hand while whispering, "You look exquisite tonight."

As compliments went, it was well done. Her initial intention was to brush the remark aside as she hurried to the basement to check her wine stock. Terri stood catty-corner to her sipping chardonnay while talking to Jeff. Her expression resembled a cross between Medusa's gaze and a sonic death ray and it rested on Donna. The woman could never stand not being the center of male admiration. Perhaps she could introduce her to Arnie, which would be another male in her admiring circle. Arnie tucked Donna's hand into his bent arm. The man assumed a great deal, which she needed to stop.

"Allow me to introduce you to the guests." She steered the man in the direction of Terri and Jeff. It was time to don her big artificial smile, which her brother referred to as *I'm pretending I like you* expression. Although to be honest, she did like some of the guests.

"Hello All, I'd like to introduce you to Arnie. Arnie, this is Jeff Ferguson."

The two men shook hands and murmured greetings of the sort. All good so far. She turned to Terri, who was the eyeing Arnie as if he were something nasty she'd accidentally stepped in, ruining her expensive shoes. *Typical.* Few were worthy of the rarefied sphere where Terri existed. Donna felt sympathy for the man since she'd spent her share of time fighting for a shred of self-worth in high school while Terri and her mean girls' clique treated her as if she deserved none.

"Terri, it might surprise you to know that Arnie has done very well for himself." She could feel the man puff up beside her. Before he could explain the nature of his business, she babbled on. "He started his own business, a butler firm. He has several employees, hundreds of clients, and is a millionaire."

Donna kept an avid watch on Terri's disinterested face as she toyed with her wine glass. When she mentioned the word *million-aire*, she looked up. It was what Donna expected. Somehow, she needed to sweeten the pot. In a daring move, she touched Terri's arm in a friendly fashion, surprised she hadn't sunk her talons into her for such effrontery.

"Arnie is amazingly still single. I imagine when the women at the reunion get a load of him there will be a line forming. Not only is he an astute businessman, but he's charming." She stopped to bestow a smile on the man while considering what else she would say. "He's handsome and a snazzy dresser, too."

That last line felt weird coming out of her mouth. The swinging door to the kitchen caught her eye as Mark emerged, holding two wine bottles. He angled his chin, giving her a questioning glance. Probably asking what she was doing with the man that Mark's presence was supposed to scare away.

"Ah, well, I'm needed elsewhere." She lifted her hand from Arnie's arm, but he covered it with his own, turning with her as she moved toward Mark. "What are you doing?" She hissed the words.

"I'll tell you what I'm not doing. No way will I even stand near that toxic woman. You may have forgotten what she was like in high school, but I haven't. She used to call me *short plug.*"

"That name makes no sense. Maybe she liked you, and that was her way of showing it."

"Please. You were there in high school. I doubted she treated you any better."

"True." Although accepting Arnie's legitimate dislike of Terri didn't make dealing with the woman any easier. "I figured you'd like her since she's still glamorous."

"Ha. That bag of bones?"

Arnie's loud voice had her looking over her shoulder to see if

Terri heard. The woman seethed and directed her death ray on the speaker.

Unaware that she could possibly burst into flames at any moment, Arnie patted her hand.

"Personally, Donna, I prefer a well-padded woman like yourself."

It might be time to zap him with her own look. The look that frightened newbie nurses and lab techs. *Well padded* her foot. She preferred the term *athletic built.*

Mark placed the newly opened bottles of wine on the server before stalking to where she and Arnie huddled to escape the glance of the basilisk. The good detective had donned his business expression, the one where people would think twice about whatever they were doing.

Mr. Babble made a beeline to the unwatched wine bottles. Donna attempted to signal Mark, who seemed unaware of the man behind him splashing wine into his oversized balloon glass. It would be the equivalent to two glasses, and she knew he'd already had his portion. All she needed was for him to feel masterful and pick a fight.

"You there," Mark drawled, "Unhand my beloved."

Beloved? Unhand? Did the man read regency romances in his spare time? It wasn't exactly what she wanted. His role was supposed to be a reassuring male presence.

Arnie gave her a questioning look before he dropped his arm. "Who's the clown?" He managed to say the words loud enough to carry. All of the sudden, she was the center of attention, and she didn't like it. Donna didn't mind when people complimented a delicious dish she made or even the inn, but she preferred not to garner the attention personally. Now, she was stuck in a farce. She threw an apologetic look at Arnie.

"You must excuse him. He's very possessive. Must come from being a detective."

Arnie's gulp was audible, and then he whispered, "Armed?"

She nodded, before drifting over to Mark and taking his arm. She turned the man toward the unwatched wine bottles where Mr. Babble was helping himself to yet another glass. "I do so appreciate your help, my sweet dumpling." She batted her eyes as they strolled closer to the bottles.

Maria stood close, rearranging the remaining savory appetizers on one plate as she picked up the empty one. She winked as she passed. "Daniel will be so disappointed that he wasn't here."

Mrs. Babble herded her complaining husband upstairs. At least something was working out in Donna's favor. "Thank goodness they're leaving. I was really regretting not having an elevator if he got any drunker."

Someone stumbled on the stairs and cursed. Mark looked in the direction of the noise. "I'll go check and make sure he makes it to his room."

"Thanks." Donna grabbed a bottle of wine, giving the guests small pours as opposed to big ones since she was unaware of everyone's drink count. As she came closer to Terri, the woman gave her a crocodile smile full of dangerous teeth.

"Give me some more of that mediocre wine."

Donna topped her glass, certain that if the woman got stinking drunk she could toss her over her well-padded shoulder and carry her upstairs. Maybe the woman would behave even more outrageously and show everyone her true colors, which was petty. She knew that, but it didn't stop her from wishing for karma to work a little faster.

"Sure, I'd love to refill your glass with this award-winning wine." Donna knew it was award-winning since she'd scoured the Internet for the best wine she could get at the most inexpensive price, which was hard to combine the two.

Heavy footsteps came down the stairs, possibly signaling Mark's return. She glanced at the stairs where Wyn stood, resplendent in a brown shirt with gold stripes that seemed to glow. Of course, the superstar would wear something eye catching.

Terri spoke beside her. "He's here."

The slight catch in her breath was movie-worthy. *Geesh, those two.* She glanced over Wyn's shoulder for a sign of the beleaguered wife, Jessica. *Nothing.* The woman was probably exhausted from toting the luggage or preferred not to witness her husband making a fool of himself trying to return to his high school glory days. At least, she'd assumed they were his glory days. For all she knew, he could be a big deal right now.

Mark appeared behind Wyn on the stairs. Wyn was as much a diva as the second shift nurse who had once been a Dallas Cowboys cheerleader. Pamela used to hesitate in a patient's doorway expecting applause. A patient wired up to the IV drip didn't dare clap. Most just wanted morphine or to go to the bathroom.

The two men standing together allowed her a tiny moment of introspection. Mark hovered a stair behind Wyn, putting him above the man, both literally and figuratively. While Wyn possessed the good looks that drew eyes, her gaze moved over Wyn briefly, but lingered on Mark. The detective maintained an attractive, weathered charm. Best of all, she knew he was a stand-up type of person, here for her when she needed him.

It wasn't too surprising she'd had a crush on Wyn in her younger days. The best thing about Wyn was his social position in the pecking order. The man could have lifted her from the nerdy crowd into the popular one with his attention. It hadn't happened, which was just as well. She didn't need Terri as a lifelong enemy. Besides, she'd be foolish enough to speak her mind, which would have gotten her promptly banned from the group. The favor of someone inside the clique only went so far.

Thank goodness Wyn had never showed more than a passing interest in her. It also allowed her to realize being in the popular group wasn't a good thing. The epiphany didn't happen immediately. It took about ten years and one school reunion where cheerleaders squeezed back into their tiny uniforms with unflattering results before it hit her.

She recognized Marvin's voice behind her. "Oh, who's the guy?"

Dean was quick to supply the information. "That's our innkeeper's main squeeze. Don't you remember he served as the wine steward tonight?"

"No, the other one. Who's standing on the stairs like Scarlett O'Hara waiting for everyone to notice him before sweeping into the ball?"

"Don't know."

Apparently, the guests thought Mark was her boyfriend. Odd, she hadn't introduced him as such. What constituted a romantic alliance? Sure, they spent time together on a regular basis without sloppy endearments or holding hands. Her eyes traveled back to the man in question, whose lips lifted in a wry grin, waiting for Wyn to make his entry.

Wyn's foot hovered in the air before hitting the next step as he proceeded down. "Greetings, friends. Forgive my tardy entrance. I had…" He paused for a second, searching for a word. "I had a few obstacles to overcome."

That's how he described his wife who objected to his association with an old girlfriend? Her eyes narrowed as Wyn paraded down the steps as if he owned the inn. Greetings, friends, a person would think the man was in some old school mystery. Of course, if he was, then a guest would go missing, which was the last thing she needed.

Mark's soft tread drew her eye. His thumb and forefinger went together in a circle indicating the Babbles had made it to their room without a fuss. Good, one less disaster waiting to happen. The detective, often sporting a slightly distracted air or a dog hair decorated jacket, didn't attract admiring eyes the way Wyn's handsome profile did. All the same, she could depend on Mark to do what he promised.

Of course, the introduction of Wyn into the group might be the tipping point for something else. Her sister-in-law waved at her from her spot near the buffet, forcing her to abandon her contemplation of the two men. She nodded at the guests as she hurried to Maria. "What's up?"

"Look." Maria's manicured hand gestured to the dwindling appetizers and the half dozen mini desserts. "Do you think I should get more?"

The platters did look picked over. Wyn stood close to Terri whispering something into her ear, causing her to shriek girlishly before placing a hand over her mouth. Ah yes, discreet they weren't. She could have done without the show.

"No." She twisted her wrist to display her watch. "We have ten minutes left. I have no intention to stretch this reception out forever."

"That's what I thought." Maria bobbed her dark head. "When it hits nine, I'll clear, which should give people a hint."

Mark strolled over, catching the last bit of conversation. He went to the various open bottles of wines, lifting them to see if they were empty. "I might as well empty the wine out of these last two bottles." His fingers wrapped around a blue Riesling bottle and a blended red.

Before he could top off any guest's glass, Donna touched his arm. "Bypass the tipsy tart. She's had enough."

Mark waggled his eyebrows, assuring her he'd heard. His route included a stop by her Santa Claus Wannabe whom Terri had abandoned when Wyn arrived on the scene. The two men conversed as her gaze roamed the room. Dean and Marvin held up their glasses when she looked at them. Herman and Eunice had their heads close together, indicating either a budding romance or a possible hearing issue. It was more likely the latter. Arnie waved, mistaking her casual survey for interest. She'd more or less abandoned him after she couldn't pawn him off on Terri, which was rather unfair since they shared a mutual dislike for the predatory female.

Maria took a sideways step to move closer, before commenting, "Looks like your admirer is heading this way."

Yeah, as if she hadn't noticed. Not what she needed with Wyn and Terri doing their best to paw each other near the stairs. Besides that, her toes hurt. Why did women have to prance around in heels when men were able to wear pretty much the same shoes they always wore? Usually comfy loafers or Oxfords with no real heels and a roomy toe box. If she hurried, she could grab a platter and head for the kitchen.

It would take her only two steps to the platter and another nineteen or twenty steps to the kitchen with the shorter steps she'd have to make in heels. Arnie moved closer in his own heeled shoes, which must be uncomfortable too. In his own way, he was a bit like her. The sympathetic musing she'd wanted to reject, but instead considered. They'd both been tortured by Terri. As bonding

connections went that one sucked. She'd spun on her heel, staggering a little at her speed and reached for a platter. The heavy glass
platter lifted and moved out of her reach.

"Let me help." Arnie held the heavy dish against his chest.

Not much she could do unless she wanted to wrestle the man.
Not exactly the image she wanted for the inn. Instead of acknowl-
edging her inner conversation, she shrugged and reached for the
mini desserts. Arnie followed her into the kitchen, making her
wonder if she should start charging people for kitchen tours.

"Thanks." She added, "I know you want to get back to the party,
not much time left and all."

He put the platter down and spoke as he moved slowly toward
her. "I have no interest in that party." His steps hardly made a
sound.

Donna turned slightly, trying to keep her eyes on the man as she
marveled how smoothly he moved. It must come in handy when
entering a yard with an angry dog that didn't take well to having his
personal deposits removed. His hands landed on her upper arms
before she'd even speculated about his intentions.

He leaned forward, his hot garlic breath blasting her face. "We
could make our own party."

The dated come-on line made her groan the same time the door
swung open. Mark backed into the kitchen carrying a tray of empty
bottles. "Well, I think that went well." He half-turned, spotted the
two of them, shoved the tray onto the counter, and immediately left.

Oh no, she knew how it looked. She lunged toward the door only
to find Arnie's hands clamped firmly on her arms, stopping her.
Without giving it too much thought, she brought her arms up in a
sharp, fast motion that broke Arnie's grip.

In the dining room, everyone had left except for Maria, who was kneeling, trying to reach an abandoned fork under the table. She looked up from her crouched position as Donna entered the room. "What did you say to Mark? He just left the inn like it was on fire."

Well, that explained his absence. "I think he had a work call." Maria gave her a glance that announced her disbelief. Lying was not part of Donna's skill set. She picked up the glass tumblers filled with clean utensils and tucked them in the buffet server. Another metal tray allowed her to gather up the dirty dishes left on the various round tables draped with ecru tablecloths.

A door closing had her looking up, hoping it would be Mark. Arnie sauntered into the room. Oh him, she'd left him in the kitchen. The man gave her a two-fingered salute. "I see you're one who likes to play hard to get," he stated, heading upstairs.

Maria's dark head swiveled to Donna. "What did that mean?"

Her concentration seesawed between what she needed to do to get ready for breakfast in the morning and Terri and Wyn's location. "Oh, I gave him the upward arm cut from defense class."

Crumbs on a tablecloth merited a tablecloth shakeout, but not inside the inn. She gathered the edges of the tablecloth as her sister-in-law chuckled. They both gathered dishes and tablecloth and headed for the kitchen.

Maria continued to snicker as she backed into the door. "I wish I saw that. Playing hard to get, huh?"

"No, I wasn't. I was doing my best not to offend a guest, which the man misinterpreted. Then Mark comes into the kitchen." She stumbled to a stop, not sure how to explain her warring feelings. "He takes one look at Arnie trying to embrace me and heads off."

"His rapid exit makes sense." Maria rested her tray near the dishwasher and opened the appliance. "Who knew you were such a femme fatale?"

"I'm not." She helped Maria sort the dishes into the dishwasher. Big plates near the outside, smaller plates in front of them. Bowl and cups in the top tray, while crystal was hand washed. "That's why I wanted to talk to Mark and explain."

"Hmm." Maria put all the forks with tines facing up, as she talked. "Might do the man good to see someone else interested in you. Men can be odd creatures, wanting a woman someone else is dating or, at least, is interested in."

"Women are just the same," she added, thinking of Terri's obsession with a married man. "Always wanting the off limits male."

"Which man is off limits? Arnie or Mark?" Maria powered up the dishwasher. Donna's hand tightened on the electric broom she kept for fast cleanup. The lightweight appliance had the ability to glide into hard to reach places. "I wasn't talking about me. Terri and Wyn, even now, may be giving my brass bed an endurance test."

"No big deal. Relax. You know you'll have plenty of guests that won't necessarily be married to each other. They look for out of the way places where they won't run into co-workers or neighbors. As long as they pay, what do you care?"

Not the image she wanted for her inn. Of course, calling it the Painted Lady meant there was bound to be misunderstandings. Her nose wrinkled as she recognized the truth of Maria's words. "You're right. I guess I never expected a guest would arrive with his wife and girlfriend."

"Ballsy," Maria admitted, while she opened a cabinet and withdrew her oversized hobo bag purse. "I'm calling it a night. I'll send Daniel to help you with breakfast. It's the least he can do since he was a no show tonight."

"I'll need him here by 8:45 since I need help with getting the plates to the tables. I couldn't make it without the two of you helping."

"Yeah, I know. Since you pay us in wine, food, and gossip, we're probably good for a couple more months until you can afford actual help. Although, you should try for some high school kid who would work for cheap."

"No teens in this neighborhood need extra money." Personally, she could pass on a chatty offspring of the influential set relating every issue that occurred inside the inn walls. "Maybe I could find someone in desperate need of what I could pay outside our local zip code." Better yet, maybe the mythical helper could sleep in the pantry, which Donna planned to do.

"Throw in at least one meal to sweeten the deal and you might find someone." Maria opened the back door and lifted a hand in goodbye. "Lock up."

Sheesh. As if she'd forget to lock up with the earlier issues she'd had with the inn being a meeting spot for criminal types, and Eunice slipping in the unlocked side door. Then there was the issue with someone stealing the backpack from her kitchen counter when she left the backdoor unlocked. The clatter of dog nails meant wherever her puggle had been taking sanctuary had just turned him out. Just as well, she slept better when her dog was near.

"Playing up to other women, huh?"

The overweight puggle plopped down near her feet and looked up at her expectantly with his large glassy eyes. She threw him a dog treat, which he snapped out of the air. Her pooch had probably spent time soothing Mrs. Babble after tucking her tipsy husband into bed. It merited an extra treat.

After arranging the spices and pans she'd need in the morning, it was time for bed. Her nightly ritual of washing her face and brushing her teeth, she did in the laundry room. A previous owner added a stool, sink, and a tiny shower in the laundry room, the facilities crowded next to a commercial washer and dryer.

Even though she expected to spend the night tossing and turning, her eyes drooped as she placed her head on the pillow. The lassitude claiming her body felt the similar to when she resorted to sleeping pills. For some reason that should be important, but she just couldn't grasp why.

Chapter Six

W ATER SPLASHED AS she poured it into the oversized coffee urn. It took the pot thirty minutes to heat up. She'd had early bird guests prowl the inn as early as seven for a cup of brew. If she had it ready along with hot water, tea fixings, and a plate of biscotti, it bought her time. Otherwise, guests kept sticking their heads in the kitchen inquiring about the possibility of coffee.

Her brother had suggested putting out some fruit, yogurt, and granola. The idea flopped after a guest complained via online review that the inn only served a measly continental breakfast. Unfortunately, the guest had left before the real breakfast happened.

Hand lettered placards on each table informed that breakfast occurred at nine a.m. Today's breakfast would be steel cut oatmeal with brown sugar and pecans, followed by Eggs Florentine. Each table also had a basket of breakfast breads, including muffins, scones, and croissants, which she baked ahead of time.

As nice as the breakfast was, she was ready for the purists who'd insist on bacon and eggs. The bacon sizzled in the oven, and it wouldn't take any time to make eggs on demand. For the vegans, she could whip up a tofu substitute. Eunice was the first to appear. She filled up her coffee cup, grabbed a couple of biscotti, and followed Donna into the kitchen.

Her first impulse was to push the inquisitive woman out. Still, she'd let her hang out in the kitchen yesterday and had set the mold for the rest of the weekend. The woman had a good eye for details. It would be nice to hear her opinion.

"Pull up a stool, Eunice."

The woman didn't wait for Donna's invitation. She slurped her coffee. "Good. Didn't get stingy with the beans."

The rough compliment pleased her as Donna centered the large cast iron skillet on the burner, uncertain if she should make hash browns to accompany the meal. Potatoes were cheap and people liked them. The only downside was the effort and time. Perhaps Eunice could help. Didn't older women know how to cook? Wasn't it a requirement or something?

Eunice bit into the biscotti, crunched for a few moments before speaking. "This cookie is dry. You left it in the oven too long. Shame. It had potential."

Forget asking Eunice for help. "It's biscotti, which is intentionally dry since it is twice baked at low temps to dry it out."

"Who'd want to do that?" The woman dunked the rest of her half-eaten biscotti into her coffee and took another bite. "Not bad if you dunk it in coffee first."

"I'll keep that in mind." Donna arranged the breakfast breads in linen wrapped baskets. She'd popped each one in the microwave for ninety seconds to warm them up. A quick peek into the oven indicated the bacon needed to be turned. With hot pad clad hands, she pulled out the bacon pan.

"You're making bacon? I would have suspected some of your guests to be vegetarians."

Great, the woman was not only a food critic but a healthy living advisor too. How could she get her out of the kitchen without using a catapult?

Eunice peered at the pan. "I love bacon! A person has to enjoy a few vices."

Okay. She'd let her stay. One of her vices might be gossip. "Did you enjoy the reception last night and meeting everyone?" Bacon flipped, she eased it back into the oven.

"Ha, I know what you're up to."

Eunice lifted her pencil-enhanced eyebrows. That meant Mark was right about her not being subtle. Before she could deny anything, Eunice answered her unspoken question. A bony index finger went up for emphasis.

"Herman asked you to feel me out. Yeah, his interest was obvious. Smart man, good conversationalist, but a little too old for me. Don't tell him until after I leave. I don't want his heart broken. In fact," she winked, "I'll play along, flirt with him, make his day. What man wouldn't be flattered to have a woman of the world return his attention?"

Donna turned toward the fridge, which allowed her to hide both her raised eyebrows and surprise. "Your secret is safe with me." The heavy cream and butter she balanced in the crook of one arm and the eggs in the other. A foot tap closed the fridge. "What did you think of the other guests?"

"Hmm," The woman cradled her head with her hand while resting her elbow on the counter. "You know Dean and Marvin are planning on opening their own bed and breakfast? They're not only buying antiques but studying you to see what you do right or wrong."

Somehow, that tarnished her former affection for the two. Of course, this all could be some crazy theory in Eunice's mind. "How do you know this?"

"They told me."

"Ah." Hard to dispute unless Eunice made it up to make conversation. It wasn't as if she'd ask the men their plans. No reason why they couldn't open their own place. "Anyone else attract your interest?"

"The man pretending to be Father Christmas? He's harmless. Someone probably mentioned his similarity to St. Nick, and he decided to capitalize on it."

The woman's summary echoed her own. Could be she underestimated the old dear. A loud belch bounced off the hanging copper bottom pots. Eunice could benefit from some etiquette lessons. "I thought the same. Anything else?"

"Do you mean the Babbles? Folks who didn't marry their soul mate and constantly snipe at each other. I've seen plenty like them, which is the reason I never married. What's your excuse?"

Donna's eyebrows almost pushed into her hairline at the unexpected question. "I never said I wasn't married. I could be."

"Yeah, right. Anyone could see no man has tamed you to the bridle. You're like me in the fact you do exactly what you please. It irritates you when people try to stop you. If you were married, I doubt your friend filling wine glasses would be helping you. Then there's the short guy clomping around in his high heeled boots trying to woo you."

Tamed to bridle she knew was horse language, but she didn't care for the sound of it. It meant that a man would determine which way she'd turn. No thank you. "So are you a horse woman?"

The woman frowned as she peered into her coffee cup. Eunice hand slapped the island surface. "Good one, yes, I'm a horsewoman. No, you didn't change the subject."

"What does it matter if I'm married or not?"

"It doesn't. I knew you weren't because you wouldn't have been so offended by the pretty boy and his floozy girlfriend if you were."

"That makes no sense." She pulled the bacon out of the oven and lifted each piece onto a paper towel draped plate. "Why would I not care if I were married?"

"Ha, glad to see you're thinking about it. One of the skills needed to be a good investigator. Let's say you were married. Your husband is at home watching sports while you circulate and flirt with the male guests."

"It's not flirting when it means nothing."

Eunice snorted her disbelief before continuing. "People do it all the time. It makes them feel attractive, but they both go home to their spouses and live their ordinary lives with a little more spring in their step."

Great heavens, the woman was starting to make sense. "Got it." A tip of the pan sent the bacon grease into a small glass container. The dirty pan went into the sink, and she retrieved another pan for the prosciutto ham. After spraying it, she arranged the paper-thin ham on the pan.

"What are you making?"

"Eggs Florentine." She expected to her to ask for more details.

"Are you going to make those thin potato pancakes to put it on top of?"

The thought of making twenty or more perfect pancakes for guests sounded more like a labor of Hercules as opposed to a doable option. "No, I'm putting it on a tomato slice just like the 'Meals in Thirty' cook on television does."

Eunice held up her hands. "I wasn't criticizing, although I'm sure some of the guests would prefer the potato pancake."

"True. Maybe they can have potatoes tomorrow. I have today's meal planned." Any uncharitable thoughts she might have had vanished with the entrance of Daniel. The sun came in with him as he swung the back door open. "How's my favorite sister?"

It was a running gag between the two of them since she was his only sister. The same blonde Nordic looks worked better on her muscular brother, than they did on her. "Amazing, considering I only got a few hours of sleep dozing on the air mattress."

"Donnie, sometimes you have to let go." He stepped into the kitchen and noticed Eunice listening intently to the conversation. He placed a hand over his heart. "Who is this vision of loveliness?"

The blatantly obvious flattery had Eunice beaming. Her brother managed to deliver the trite compliment with such sincerity the woman swallowed it whole. Perhaps he could give her a course on charm, although it would probably fall flat for her since she didn't have the male physique to go with it. Something about a handsome man caused women to check their intelligence. It would fall to her to introduce her besotted guest.

"This is Eunice. She's a guest who also happens to be a sleuth."

Daniel looked intrigued, which resulted in Eunice sitting up straighter, taking off about ten years from her appearance. "That I am."

"Wonderful. I will love to hear about it. Let me grab some coffee, first." He slipped into the dining room, making Donna wonder if he forgot his true purpose was to help her. The sound of voices from the dining room indicated not only had other guests drifted downstairs, but Daniel was charming them. A glance at her watch indicated it was past time to start the eggs. She'd prefer to do them as the guests arrive, but unfortunately, they often arrived in a pack.

A *ting* signaled the oatmeal was finished. The rice cooker did double service for oatmeal.

"What's that?" Eunice looked around her for the source of the noise.

Donna carefully lifted out the large commercial pan, trying not to slosh it. The eggs she poached last night floated in the water. By placing the pan on the burner, and gradually heating the eggs, it would make them warm throughout without cooking them more. Once she had the pan centered on the burner, she could answer her inquisitive guest. "Oatmeal."

"Yuck! I thought this was supposed to be a highbrow place with a decent breakfast. Wouldn't have booked here if I knew you were going to pass off gruel as food." The woman's puckered face indicated she wasn't a fan.

"Eunice," she used her name, relying on her nurse's training that the use of a person's name made them relax, "I understand you've probably experienced slimy, grey, overcooked oatmeal."

"Every day of my childhood, since my Scottish granny cooked it. Flavorless stuff she insisted would stick to my ribs."

"I understand, but what I'm making is nothing like that. The steel cut oats hold their texture and compliment the butter, brown sugar, cinnamon, and pecans. Why don't you try a small taste?"

Eunice cocked her head as if trying to decide if Donna was joking. "Small one."

Donna snagged a custard dish and ladled a large spoonful into it. She added in the butter, sugar, nuts, and spices and gave it a good stir before handing it to Eunice who acted as if she'd received arsenic. Even though she didn't have time to waste, Donna watched Eunice take the first bite. Her sour face transformed into surprise, then, bliss. She scraped the bowl clean and held it out for a refill.

This was why she opened The Painted Lady Inn. If she could transform people's lives with a delicious bowl of oatmeal or the perfect scone, then she was content. She heaped more oatmeal in the small bowl while asking, "So what do you think?"

"Tolerable." The woman admitted with the slightest hesitation in her voice.

Ha, she heard it. The tough old bird was stingy with compliments, but before the weekend was over, she'd pry one out of her.

Daniel came back through the door with his coffee. "We have four up. The Babbles at one tabletop. A man named Ferguson who looks like…"

"Santa," Eunice and Donna chorused together.

"Yeah." Her brother grinned before continuing. "Then there's Arnie, who told me he was your special friend. When I told him I was your brother, he looked relieved. Told me he didn't need any more competition and hoped we'd be on good terms since we might end up related."

Eunice whooped. "Mercy, you work fast."

Donna's hand landed on two breadbaskets, which she stuffed into the microwave before turning to ladle up four bowls of oatmeal. She rolled her eyes, not sure why she attracted Arnie. Apparently, her disinterest served as an aphrodisiac.

"No worries. No chance on the two of you becoming related unless he has an unattached relative."

Daniel laughed and withdrew the bread when the microwave pinged. She put the four steaming bowls of oatmeal on a wood tray. She placed a dollop of butter in each bowl, then, shook the brown sugar and cinnamon mixture over it, finishing it with a small cup of pecans on the side for those who didn't like nuts.

With the tray hoisted against her belly, she nodded to Daniel. It was time to serve the first wave of customers. She'd prefer not to go out with her apron on, but she didn't have time to change. Daniel headed toward Mr. Ferguson first, which caused her to veer in the direction of the Babbles, who were much more subdued this morning. Could be the man suffered from a hangover. The woman, however, leaned back to look around her. If the woman was ogling her brother in front of her husband, then she was bold.

"Where's Jasper?" *Ha*, her brother would be taken down a notch to realize Jasper usurped him.

"He's a late sleeper. He'll be up and around before breakfast is over."

No need to add she locked him in the basement to keep him from being underfoot in the chaos that usually consisted of breakfast preparation. He did have a bed in the basement though, and he could be sleeping.

Mrs. Babble put her hands together. "I can't wait."

"I bet Jasper can't, either." The remark, which she meant more for herself, caused the woman to beam. Maybe she had this small talk thing down pat. She could utter her regular sarcastic thoughts, but with a pleasant countenance.

"Hope you like *gourmet* oatmeal." She centered a bowl in front of *Santa*.

"I do, especially with buttered toast." He grinned up at her.

Message received. She needed to put the rush on toast. Too bad Eunice couldn't help if she insisted on hanging in the kitchen. One more bowl and she'd be free to finish to her next dish. Daniel would have to attend to the next group on his own.

Arnie sat at the corner table watching her the way a cat would an especially unobservant bird. The difference was she knew he was there. *Drop the bowl and go.* The good thing about Arnie, no matter how abrupt she was, he'd interpret it into something positive.

"Good morning, here's your scrumptious oatmeal." She placed the oatmeal on the table when she heard Mark's voice in the hallway. *Good*, she needed to talk to him. She dangled the now empty tray from one hand. Half-turned, she stretched her neck to see into the hallway. Daniel's broad shoulders blocked out most of Mark, but she could see he had flowers in one hand. *Flowers?* Without being told she knew they were for her. *She couldn't remember the last time she received flowers, especially if she discounted the time the florist mis-delivered a bouquet to her house for Mother's Day.*

The scrape of the chair legs on wood served as a warning as Arnie leapt to his feet and planted a noisy kiss on her cheek. If she hadn't jerked her head back, it may have landed on her lips. "Why did you do that?"

"Following instructions."

"What instructions?" She hoped Mark hadn't witnessed that display. Dean and Martin had because they commented loudly enough for everyone to hear.

"That must be some breakfast."

Arnie took his seat, looking a little chagrinned but not much. With her luck, he probably preferred bossy women. "Your apron told me to do it."

Since when did she have a talking apron? Her holiday one had a blinking Rudolph on it. A quick glance downward revealed she was wearing a *Kiss the Cook* apron. Well, she'd have to change, but the memory of her eggs gently warming sent her darting back to the kitchen. As she jogged past her brother, she noticed he was holding the roses she'd seen in Mark's hand earlier.

Daniel followed her into the kitchen and placed the roses on the counter, "Who knew fifty was the year you'd knock over men as if they were bowling pins?"

Eunice made some noise under her breath. Donna suspected it was a sound of derision. Right now, she had Eggs Florentine to worry about. "Put some toast in the toaster for Father Christmas. I have to deal with the sauce."

Eunice picked up the flowers. "I'll take care of these. Any vases?"

Donna sautéed the onions while pointing to the end cabinet with her left hand. "Bottom door."

"Pink roses…" Eunice spoke as she grabbed kitchen shears from the knife block, causing Donna to do a double take, "can mean thank you, sympathy, grace, or gladness."

Nothing that said he was interested in her as more than a friend. The flowers didn't even symbolize forgiveness. Why did he even bother to bring them? "Did Mark say anything when he dropped off the flowers?"

"Yeah, he did." Daniel buttered the toast, cut it into triangles, and placed it on a bird-decorated plate. The plates were a nice marriage of contemporary and Victorian.

Eunice caught her eyes and shook her head, as if to say *men.*

Her brother disappeared behind the door without elaborating. *Great.* She'd forgotten the juice and milk. She pulled out a tray of old-fashioned glass milk bottles filled with various juices and milk. Her brother could carry it out on his next trip.

"Need a bread basket and oatmeal for your antiquing friends." Daniel announced as he came through the door.

Of course, she saw them, but Arnie's unexpected actions had sent her fleeing to the kitchen. She could blame it on breakfast, which was part of it. People came for food, not to watch Arnie aggressively pursue her. Her life had turned into a made for television movie that she'd laugh at if it were happening to someone else.

"I think you can handle it." Her focus was on cutting the beef-steak tomatoes into exactly one-half inch thick slices. Normally, she insisted on doing most of the food herself, making sure the presentation was flawless. Presentation was fifty percent of the meal and sometimes more, depending on what was being served.

"Are you sure?" Daniel's voice carried doubt.

Eunice quit clipping the flowers and shouldered her brother out of the way. "I'll do it. I watched her."

Donna mentally lectured herself about broken rules by allowing a guest to assist as she spooned the sauce over each tomato. She placed a poached egg on top of the sauce, and then crumbled crispy ham over it. One down, her plan was to serve them in twos to prevent the eggs from going cold. "Two eggs up."

No Daniel. He must be serving the oatmeal. Unfortunately, her brother could be involved in conversation on an esoteric topic. The eggs were ready to go out, and she didn't need to abandon the stove or encounter Arnie again. Eunice bustled by her and picked up the plates. "Babbles. They were first down."

She plated two more eggs by the time Daniel and Eunice returned. Daniel spotted the tray of bottles, grabbed them, and disappeared behind the swinging door.

"Any more guests down?"

"Yeah, the vixen is down and purring up a storm. Not hard to figure out what she did last night."

That meant another bowl of oatmeal and breadbasket.

"Two more eggs up."

Daniel appeared in time for her to hand him the plates.

Eunice stood near the oatmeal, possibly waiting for instructions. "Got any saltpeter?"

"No. Why would I need that?" She hurried over to the oatmeal before Eunice could. No telling what the woman would do. Was she being pranked and all the unusual guests were part of some reality program Daniel had somehow set her up to star in? If so, there would be retribution.

She dipped up the oatmeal, added extra sugar and butter, stirred it in, and then added more. The pecans she put in a clear shot glass. Eunice could deliver it.

Fifteen minutes later, she'd served almost everyone and had five eggs left, one for Eunice, two for Wyn and his wife, and two for Daniel and herself.

"Ready to eat, Eunice? I certainly appreciate your help. I couldn't have done it without you."

The woman polished her nails on her blazer. "I know. I was wondering if you could comp my bill for my help."

She should have seen that one coming, but she hadn't. "Will do. I could knock off thirty dollars."

"I was thinking more like a day?"

Before Donna could point out even the waiters in five-star restaurants weren't paid that well, Jessica poked her head in the doorway.

"Sorry to bother you, but I can't find Wyn."

Donna was tempted to say something about her checking Terri's bed, but she didn't. Her head swiveled to pin Eunice with a look. The woman could be very free with her observations.

Eunice shrugged, and then commented, "Maybe he went for a walk."

Good save. "Yes," Donna added. "The area around the inn is very scenic and peaceful. I'm sure he'll be back soon. Why don't you sit down and have breakfast?"

The woman's shoulders were up around her ears as if steeling herself for a massive wallop. Being married to Wyn had to be a special kind of hell. At one time, the wife probably thought she netted a catch, only to discover she should have thrown him back.

Donna loaded the waiting wife's breadbasket with cheese and apple pastries. She also gave her twice the normal amount of pecans. Couldn't do anything about her poor choice in husbands, but she could give her a luxuriant breakfast.

The real question was when Wyn showed up would it turn into a scene?

Chapter Seven

AFTER THE COMMOTION of serving everyone, the empty kitchen functioned as a haven. Donna sat down to eat breakfast with Daniel. Her brother sliced into his Eggs Florentine. "Sis, I'm not sure why you have to add spinach to everything." He popped a bite into his mouth and chewed. "This is surprisingly good."

He always acted surprised when she cooked up something tasty. To be fair, she hadn't cooked much when they grew up together. How would he know she could cook until she did? Most of the meals they shared were at restaurants. "Eunice liked it, too. Even the oatmeal, which she called tolerable."

"Yeah, she's a hoot, but she pitched in and helped."

"I'm grateful, even reminded me to put out the bacon. Of course, she wants me to comp her room for today. Wouldn't be surprised if she shows up tomorrow to help." It might be some scam the woman works by staying at various inns and offering to help to defray her bill. "Not really sure why she showed up in Legacy."

"Could be lonely and picked our fair city."

"It seems unlikely, but an extra pair of hands came in handy with Arnie being crazy and Jessica misplacing her husband."

She savored her own breakfast while creating a mental to-do list. Couldn't clean up the rooms until the people left. No one had, so she might as well restock the snack pantries on each floor.

"What's this about a misplaced husband?" Daniel held up a

finger. "I'm going to get more coffee. You need any?"

She pushed her almost empty cup in his direction. Dirty dishes littered almost every surface. It would take at least three cycles to get all the dishes done. The thought made her wilt a little on her stool. While she suspected innkeeping would be hard, the reality bore no resemblance to her fantasies, where she flitted around in a clean apron surrounded by euphoric guests praising her culinary efforts. There were enough high points from satisfied guests, glowing reviews, and perfect entrees to keep her going through the last twelve months.

Could she interest someone in working for almost nothing? She could offer room and board if she could get her brother to frame up a small room in the storage area and finish the laundry room facilities whenever his construction schedule allowed.

Daniel returned with the filled cups, placing one in front of Donna.

"Thanks." She picked up her cup as she considered the possibility of help. "If you boxed up a tiny bedroom in the back room and a bathroom in the laundry room, what type of person could I get to live there? He or she would have to work for almost no money."

Her brother appeared thoughtful and didn't laugh outright as she thought he would.

"College student, a man or woman going through a divorce, someone starting over for whatever reason. What you need is a cheerful, capable person in dire circumstances."

"That's all?" He made it sound easy and even doable.

Daniel angled his head toward the door. "Tell me about the misplaced husband?"

Her eyes cut to the door, aware someone could be in the hall, as she lowered her voice. "I suspect the wife knows exactly where her husband is. He's in bed sleeping off his romp with his old flame that he told to stay at my inn."

"Reunion crowd?" Daniel had the nerve to smirk.

"Yes." While she expected some people might want to renew old friendships, she didn't expect them to do it on her sheets.

"Hmm." He scratched his head as he pondered the dilemma. "Well, you have to expect such shenanigans. Same thing goes on in other accommodations. The difference is the inn is small enough for you to notice."

"You're right. I keep expecting some big scene, but despite this feeling I have here," her cupped hand tapped her chest, "I'm sure there won't be one. Anyone married to Wyn accepts him for who he is, or she'd divorce him. Still, his wife surprises me."

"Why?"

Good question, which she'd dwelled on more than she should have. "She's a quiet, smoldering woman probably ready to explode dealing with the husband's antics. I'd expect a female version of Wyn. Someone over the top." Donna used her hands to swerve in and out indicating an hourglass shape.

"Would she have gobs of blonde curls?"

"Yes and if she's close to Wyn's age, she'll do the full makeup believing that it somehow makes her look younger."

"Look out the window at the woman getting out of the taxi."

She stood and turned to peer out their extra tall window. The lace panel provided shielding, but not too much. How weird that a woman she'd just describe would suddenly appear. Even odder, she was walking toward the inn. "Strange."

The bell sounded. Daniel walked to the door, bumping into her as she stood. "I'll get this," he volunteered.

When it came to delivering bad news, such as no vacancy, her brother did it better. After a prolonged conversation, the person would wander off happy and bemused. She tended to be more abrupt, by stating the place was full.

The woman's raised voice penetrated the kitchen door. "I'm Wyn's wife."

The uncomfortable tightness she'd felt in her chest upon waking returned full force. It looked like she was going to get the scene after all. Donna pushed open the door, knowing she needed to rescue her brother. While he generally charmed women, angry women were his kryptonite. Her nursing job brought her in close contact with irate women who were mad at the world for their own mortality or a beloved family member's.

"Can I help you?"

Donna wished she had her heels on so she could stare the woman in the eye. The woman's platform shoes gave her the height edge. Instead, she had to cant her head upward as if she were a kindergartener.

"Are you the floozy my husband took up with?"

Movement at the edge of her peripheral vision caused her to dip her head enough to see Jessica easing back up the steps. She'd never have credited Jessica with being the other woman. Oh yeah, she forgot to answer, but her brother did it for her.

"You're talking to my sister, who owns the inn. She's no one's floozy."

Arnie chose to walk down the steps at that moment. Most people witnessing a scene in progress would have the good sense to return to their room, but not Arnie.

"Hey, don't talk about my sweetheart like that."

Daniel gave her a shocked look. She could only answer with a shrug. The more she was around Arnie the more she was convinced the man might not be entirely stable.

The woman pivoted and pinned Arnie with a laser gaze the man didn't wilt under. He did have the good sense to stay on the fourth step. It was far enough away in case the woman lunged. It also gave him the advantage of being taller.

"Who are you?"

"Arnie Forrester, earnest suitor of Donna Tollhouse."

The woman snorted. "Yeah, Wyn used to talk about me that way." She glanced back in Donna's direction. "Don't be taken in. At first, he couldn't live without me. Now he's sneaking off to play slap and tickle with another female."

The slap and tickle she'd agreed was spot on, but Arnie and Wyn being the same didn't ring true. "Ah, ma'am,…" She hesitated, wondering how she'd fix this problem.

"Name's Lucinda."

That sounded about right. "Your husband isn't here. He never showed for breakfast. I suspect he went for a walk. He possibly could have headed back home to your loving arms."

Lucinda gave her a narrowed eye look. "You better not be covering up for some husband stealer."

"I'm not."

Lucinda didn't look convinced. The woman would probably want to search each room forcing Donna to call the police. "Perhaps you'd like to take a walk around the grounds. There's a nice boardwalk near the bay."

Her brother offered his arm. "I'd be glad to show you around."

Lucinda looked at Donna, studying her face before murmuring her agreement. She could hear her talking as they left. "Wyn would be so jealous seeing me with such a handsome man."

She certainly hoped so, resulting with the two of them jumping into a car and racing home. It also meant Terri and Jessica would leave early, although the fine print specified reservations changed less than forty-eight hours would result in a zero refund.

The door shut, reminding her that her clean-up help just left. A desperate college student would come in handy about now. She'd have to interview everyone, which might allow her to sniff out the partiers and slackers.

"Can I help?" She'd forgotten about Arnie. The fact she could amazed her. "No, I don't think so unless you want to do dishes."

"Okay. Sounds good to me"

The day kept getting more peculiar. "No, you don't have to."

Arnie descended the steps and joined her. "No issues. I do dishes at home."

"Not this many. Mostly it's scraping, loading the machine, unloading and putting away." She didn't expect him to help her, but part of her coveted the help if he really meant it.

"I can do that. I think it is the least I could do, considering I may have messed up things with you and your beau."

She almost asked whom but realized he meant Mark. "True." Still, this might be one of those sneaky techniques where the man pretends to help to get close to a woman, even if it would be hard faking doing dishes.

"Think of it as penance since my poems had everyone calling you *Hot Momma*."

He did owe her for that. "I think two years of solid dishwashing should make up for that."

"I might be able to offer you a couple of hours."

"I'll take it."

★

ARNIE, DRAPED IN a checked apron, made a good assistant. He did whatever she asked with a smile even though she knew he was trying to make a good impression on her. Jasper's whining caused her to swing into action.

"I forgot my dog." She darted in the direction of the basement to release her pup. Jasper lunged toward the back door his nails scrambling across the linoleum. She swung open the door for her pooch, but remained since he'd want back in as soon as she walked away from the door.

Arnie slipped up behind her and placed his hands on her shoulders. "I'd do your yard for free."

The idea of the man patrolling the yard with a pooper scooper amused her. "I have to say that is probably the most creative offer I've ever received."

"Yeah, real romantic, but I have to try harder."

Jasper ran up to the door, tail wagging and tongue lolling out of his mouth. Donna opened the door slowly, allowing her dog time to back up to avoid being hit. The dog darted into the house and headed for the stairs. "He's headed to the Babbles room to do his surrogate dog therapy."

They both returned to the kitchen. Arnie stacked the dried dishes while she mixed up some cookie dough. "Okay. I'd like to be clear on this. I do have a romantic interest in a local man. You saw him. That said I'm curious as to why you have to work so much harder."

He cocked his head and gave her the same disbelieving look Eunice had given her earlier.

"What? Obviously, you're a successful businessman. You're helpful. Last night, in your tuxedo, you had that James Bond thing going on." She'd crossed her fingers on that last one.

"Well, two out of three might be true. But, I'm short. How tall are you?"

"I'm five-seven." She didn't see what that had to do with any-thing.

"That's what I thought. I'm five-seven, too. That's even with my one and half inch growth spurt in college. Women want nothing to do with short men. Some study done at Duke University discovered a man had to make $40,000 for every inch under 5'10". It was a hardscrabble to make it to dog butler millionaire and still women don't take me seriously. Other people complain about dealing with crap to get where they are. I can say it and not be speaking figura-tively." He winked, making his moment of self-revelation into a joke.

The melon baller wasn't working as well as it should. A good whack on the counter should loosen it up. Pause in the conversation, which meant she should say something. "Yeah, I know what you mean."

Arnie made some snorting noise, which meant her reply didn't fit. He was talking about women rejecting him because he wasn't tall. Her lips twisted as she rejected a pithy remark to keep trying. "I wonder if they found Wyn."

"Wyn." Arnie grimaced. "Guys like him don't need to do any-thing noteworthy, but women fall all over him because he's tall."

Good looking, too, but Donna decided not to point that out.

"He's not a nice person. Not sure if you realize that. He disgusts me." He threw down the dishtowel, definitely a sign the man was not a Wyn fan.

If she mistakenly thought Wyn was some choirboy, three wom-en fighting over him would convince her otherwise. Donna kept scooping cookie dough, certain that most of Arnie's comments were rhetorical and a way to let off steam about the absent man. Arnie paced the width of the kitchen. His shoulders were tight as he grumbled about the treatment of the shorter than average male. The man hadn't even showed up at the reunion, and he was already struggling against the riptide of regret.

"Not sure what Wyn does. I doubt he ever had to work as hard as I did. There were rumors about him at school playing jokes on girls pretending to like them. Then he and Terri would laugh about how gullible the girls were."

Is that what happened to her? Her hand hung suspended in the air. She never thought of herself as one of those foolish girls who believed an invitation to dance equated a smitten male. At the time, she was euphoric since Wyn was the *Big Deal* at school. Even though she'd considered herself half in love with the man, she wasn't. What she coveted more was the position of being by his side. It never happened.

"I was one of those girls. He asked me to dance at one of the formals. Then Terri hounded me endlessly the rest of the year." Her naivety at that time made her wince as she finished the pan and slid it into the hot oven.

"No, I think you're wrong. I think he did like you."

Her cell phone rang before she could tell Arnie not to patronize her by making up stuff that wasn't true. She accepted long ago that she was only a player in a game she didn't fully understand.

The screen flashed a photo of her brother. "Hello…What? I can't hear you."

Her brother's voice, sounding strained, said, "We found him."

Static filled the line, demonstrating he was at the edge of phone reception. "You found Wyn?"

"Yes, not exactly in the condition I expected."

Weird. She hoped Daniel hadn't found Wyn in the arms of another woman, especially with his actual wife present.

"What?"

"He's gone."

"Huh? I thought you told me you found him."

"I did. He's dead."

"Oh no!" A sharp crackle of static had her pulling the phone away from her ear for a second, and then Daniel's voice came back.

"I tried to call 911, but I couldn't get the operator to understand me. Maybe you could call Taber. You can lead him to the copse of woods where we used to play explorer."

"I will."

She put the phone down with fear racing through her body like a large metal pinball, careening wildly, hitting every panic center. This couldn't be happening again.

Arnie placed a hand on her arm. "What is it?"

It hadn't escaped her notice that he took every opportunity to touch her. She should mention it, but now wasn't the time. "Wyn's dead. Daniel wants me to call Mark since I can lead him to where they are. It was an old childhood haunt of ours and isn't accessible by car."

The stretch of trees with a meandering creek cutting through it would take on an entirely different meaning for her. At least, the man hadn't died in her inn. Her thumb depressed the three on her speed dial. As she waited for the phone to ring, her better self pointed out she only thought of the man's death in how it related to her inn's reputation. Guilt sat on her left shoulder, weighing it down and causing her to list to one side. Mark picked up on the first ring.

"Hey, Donna. Glad you called. I know I've been acting like a horse's..."

As much as she wanted his explanation, she needed to deal with

Wyn first. Her free hand trembled as she sucked in a breath trying to make sense of the events herself. "Hold that thought. One of my guests is dead."

"The jerk who was kissing you."

"No, he's fine. It's Wyn Lansing. Daniel just walked out with his real wife to calm her down."

"I thought he only had one wife, Maria."

She closed her eyes for a second, trying to control the incipient panic welling up in her. Forget mentally counting to ten, she settled for five, and then took a deep, calming breath.

"He does. I meant Wyn. He arrived with one woman who wasn't his wife, and then another woman shows up claiming to be his wife. Daniel took that one for a walk. They found him—Wyn—out where Daniel and I used to play. He asked me to call you and explain the location and maybe you could relay the information."

"All right. I'll notify the EMTs and the local boys and swing by to pick you up. Everyone can follow us."

Close to her elbow, Arnie volunteered, "I'll finish the cookies for you and clean up."

Mark's voice sounded in her ear. "Who was that?"

"A guest." She didn't want to say anymore and jinx the apology she hadn't totally received. Maybe that was selfish when Wyn was lying dead. Apparently, the man had several apologies he never bothered rendering.

"I bet it's Hot Lips. He's making nice by helping you. It's the oldest trick in the book to get on a woman's good side."

"I'll keep that in mind. Hurry. Daniel doesn't do well with hysterical women. Not sure why he even took her that far away."

Mark hung up without saying anything, although it could be the call dropped. It would take a few minutes for him to arrive at least, time enough to pull out the first batch of cookies and put in the next.

Arnie propped himself against the counter and crossed his ankles. "Who do you think killed him?"

Donna picked up a hot pad and slapped his arm with it. "Stop that talk. He could have died from natural causes."

"Okay." Arnie wrinkled his nose. "You sure can be feisty. Something I suspected, but never knew for sure. Answer me this—why did he wander such a distance to die?"

"I have no clue."

Another question was when did he do it? Jessica came down looking for him at breakfast. Donna was almost sure he had visited Terri in the night by the woman's behavior this morning. She did everything but announce she was hungry after a busy night. Even ate the oatmeal without complaining, which was bizarre in itself.

The one thing she did know was she didn't need the guests gossiping about this. A few might even leave. Damage control was imperative. If a guest were a killer, then he or she wouldn't know Wyn had been discovered. The remote location almost insured the man wouldn't have been found for days, possibly weeks. She drew in a deep breath wondering how to handle things.

Arnie regarded her with a palpable tension. Perhaps he knew about the death. The only way he would was if he'd killed him.

She went for the ambush technique since she didn't have time to think up anything else. "Did you murder Wyn?"

"No. I have no reason to. I'm surprised you asked. If I were tempted to kill someone it would more likely be Terri."

Her open hand went up in a stop motion, hoping to stem all talk of killing. "Okay, that's good enough for me. You're in charge until I get back. You can put out cookies. I'm hoping most of the people go somewhere. Say nothing of what you know."

Arnie gave her a two-finger salute and clicked his heels together. She wanted to point out that type of behavior kept him single more than his lack of height.

Her vigil near the window allowed her to spot Mark's sedan. Donna was down the steps and onto the sidewalk before he parked. Mark leaned over and opened the door for her.

"Jump in, I expect more than what you told me on the phone." He pulled out into the street, leading a silent ambulance and squad car. The dog walkers stopped to stare. *Oh great*, Harry and Odell, plus their oversized poodle Gem, watched as if a parade were passing. Harry, the taller of the two, cupped his hand against his forehead shielding his eyes.

Yeah, that's right, Donna Tollhouse is in the car with the detective. Hope you notice I voluntarily got into the car on my own. A romantic attachment would explain why the good detective spent so much time at the inn.

Mark tapped her arm. "What happened?"

"Seriously, I think the man had a heart attack trying to prove to a trio of women that he was still in high school. What I don't understand was why he traveled so far from the inn?"

Chapter Eight

THE SEDAN TRADED the smooth paved roads for pitted streets with crumbling shoulders. A derelict factory stood on one side of the road. Its broken windows reminded Donna of someone with patched and broken glasses. At one time, it had been a shirt factory employing a third of the town. Textiles went overseas, leaving the town to scramble for any commerce they could get, which resulted in their Columbus Re-enactment Days. The town also hosted an Autumn Trails festival and Christmas trains.

Legacy had made a hard grab for the tourism dollar like so many other defunct manufacturing towns. As long as a person avoided this part of town, they could forget about the town's origins. Most of the teenagers had never heard about the Legacy Mills, which the town was named after. They probably assumed the town always had a dozen antique stores and an equal amount of quirky coffee shops, hemmed in by ice cream parlors and distinctive bistros. Now, they had a Victorian B and B-if she could keep it open.

The side view mirror demonstrated that the ambulance and patrol car still kept pace, despite her erratic directions that included *turn here, no back there, you missed it.* Mark cleared his throat. "You said something about you and Daniel playing around here?"

"We did. Our house was only a couple of streets over and most of this area was woods. It definitely looks different. There's an empty lot where the 'Smiling Irishman' hawked cars. We can park there."

The tall grass almost hid it except for a well-worn patch that indicated a popular short cut. It was hard to imagine anyone walking through the lot since nothing existed on this stretch of road, except for memories.

Mark bumped up into the lot, mowing down grass in the process. Once the car stopped, Donna placed her hand on the door to get out, but a firm grasp on her arm stopped her.

"Be careful. As you can see, there's broken glass everywhere." The sunlight bounced off the fragments.

"Wow, you'd think people would have something better to do than break bottles."

Daniel and she used to play *explorer* in the woods. More correctly, Daniel pretended to be some intrepid adventurer while she kept an eye on him as her parents had instructed. As a kid, he had no clue her job was to watch over him. Instead, Daniel assumed his older sister wanted to hike through the tall grass while her legs provided sustenance for the chiggers. Broken bottles weren't an issue then. People used to collect bottles for the money they'd get for returning them.

"Got the right shoes on?" Mark asked, trying to peer at her feet in the shadow under the dashboard.

Since she'd be tromping through the woods, Donna had slipped on her athletic shoes. "These will work. Do you think they can get the gurney down there?" She motioned to across the road where shabby pines and an oversized holly tree stood.

"They'll have to carry it, but I've seen the EMTs handle worse."

Donna looked affectionately at his hand resting on her arm, then up at his concerned face. "I think I can manage not to step on any glass." Mark was trying to look out for her, which was nice. Too bad the circumstances weren't better. The gesture pleased her.

Mark dropped his hand, vaulted out of the car, and made it to her side of the car by the time she opened the door to exit. The passenger door didn't swing open as freely as the driver side did, probably due to disuse.

"Donna, be careful where you step, there's bound to be hypodermic needles around here that would pierce your shoes with enough pressure."

Her eyes dropped to his sturdy brogans that would be significantly more difficult for a used, and possibly infected, needle to pierce. Okay, he won the suitable shoe battle. While she wasn't the fussiest person in the world, she'd credit Wyn with being even more fastidious. The man she knew expected the best and would have no reason to creep down to the abandoned section of town that only junkies visited. Every business had fled the area. Not even a convenience store overcharging for gas, junk food, and a big gulp drink was present.

A young patrolman spoke to Mark. "The paramedics want to know if they should bring their gurney."

"Yes. If Daniel Tollhouse said the man is dead, then he is."

The words pleased Donna, not that Wyn was dead, but Mark had such faith in her brother. She'd only hope he'd say the same thing about her.

The young cop shuffled behind her, signaling his impatience. Irritation nudged her at the officer's willingness to get the incident over with and on to something else. Her work as a nurse put her in daily contact with death, but it still packed a punch whenever she encountered it.

People died all the time from disease, heart attacks, and occasionally accidents. It could be the passing years, but each one reminded her of her immortality making her uncomfortable.

Please, don't let it be a murder. She offered up the words as a form of silent prayer, but knew they were useless.

"When are we getting started, Detective Taber?"

Ah, the young officer again, who was waiting on her to show him the way. Donna stared at the patch of trees. Behind them, the land dipped into a forgotten stretch of woods. Back in the early days, the landowner had held off various people who wanted to build a business on his land. Perhaps he wanted a bit of nature at his back door. Little did he know the woods would become a place where people would conduct activities best unwitnessed. Many a young couple slipped off into the wooded thicket for a romantic moment with a blanket and a cheap bottle of wine.

Why would Daniel walk in this direction with Lucinda who had *high maintenance* stamped all over her? Better yet, what propelled Wyn down the same path in the dark? He had to have snuck out after ten p.m. or later since she was still setting up the kitchen for breakfast until then. The only way she would discover anything was to examine the area. Wyn could have gone for a simple stroll, feeling hemmed in by all his various assignations, stumbled, hit his head. Yeah, that's what happened. Satisfied with her explanation, she put up her hand to motion across the street.

"This way." She felt a bit like an adventurer herself, leading a team into the forest.

Mark barked out an order. "Look sharp. Do not step on any footprints. Walk on the leaves and avoid anything that looks like poison ivy."

While his instructions made sense, they unsettled her. "You make it sound like you think Wyn was killed."

"Could be. Won't know until we get there. Can't undo stomping across evidence, though. Once it's compromised, we can't put it back together. Better to be safe than sorry. The order was more for the medics."

The sun penetrated the tree branches, throwing dappled light on the worn dirt path. A bird sang overhead as Donna carefully kept to the edge of the walkway. This spot of undeveloped land had a certain natural charm to it, if she ignored the occasional crumpled beer can and fast food wrapper. Five pairs of feet plus a gurney crashing through the woods destroyed the peaceful atmosphere and signaled their location.

The land sloped downward, and one of the medics cursed as he blundered into a wild berry bush. Yep, they definitely destroyed the calm. Another copse of hardwood trees shielded the stream that had kept her brother fascinated for hours. In the spring, he'd observe the development of tadpoles into frogs. It surprised her when he went into construction considering his obsession with nature.

"I think Daniel must have led Lucinda down here because he believes nature is a tranquilizer. The woman was upset when she arrived since she was on the trail of a cheating husband." It all started to come together now. Even she had to admit that her brother had a way about him that made people trust him. It was fortunate the man never opted for a life of crime.

"It would take more than a few saplings and a bunch of wild flowers to ease a female in a full out hissy fit," Mark commented to himself or possibly the cop following.

Her nose wrinkled at the comment, and she gave Mark a hard glance, which caused him to chuckle.

"Yeah, just checking to see if you were listening. I know you would never throw a hissy fit. You'd be more likely to floor someone with a left jab or a frying pan."

Her foot slid on the mud, demanding her attention, which prevented her from answering. The comment painted her as a brawler. She'd object if it weren't true.

"Down here." Daniel's familiar voice rang out.

A feminine voice joined his. "Hurry, hurry, it's horrible." A definite tinge of emotion filled the words.

Apparently, her brother hadn't been good at calming her down. Still, confronting a cheating husband and discovering a dead husband was a world of difference. It always amazed her how people could be cursing a spouse's name, then the minute something bad happened, the no good spouse became a virtual saint.

The paramedics pushed through the underbrush, past Donna and Mark. The cop lunged after them, yelling, "Don't touch anything!"

Mark ran too, muttering to himself, "No one ever listens," as he ran through a clump of poison ivy.

Or looks, she couldn't help adding, as she skirted the noxious plant and caught up with the rest of the group. The six of them stood silently beside the meandering creek. Donna could just make out Wyn's legs half on the rocky bank. Her breath caught in her throat, never quite making it out. The entire purpose of leading the authorities here was to find Wyn. Still, seeing his legs made it real.

The crowd hid the rest of him. She slid up to the edge of the group, making eye contact briefly with her brother before looking at Wyn. Her held breath went out in a whoosh. Her knees felt weak, making her wobble slightly, before she stiffened them. This was no time to get faint hearted.

The man had on a pair of chinos, expensive moccasin shoes, no socks, and a windbreaker. His hair was perfect while his face was nose first in the stream. Anyone having a heart attack or stroke would have turned his head to the side at least.

The cop pulled out a camera and snapped pictures, causing Lucinda to object.

"What is wrong with you? Are you some morbid creep?" The angry woman ran at the police officer, tackling him and taking the two of them down. Daniel jumped into action, offering his hand to pull up the raging widow. Mark squatted next to the cop. A few quick sidesteps brought Donna within hearing range.

"Ignore it, Wells. I don't think she was assaulting an officer, just shock." Wells, which must be the cop's name, mumbled something she couldn't hear. The paramedics broke through the brush holding the gurney as if it was a shield. Mark straightened up and nodded to Wells, who stood and went back to photo snapping.

The taller medic called out, "Certain about the death?"

"Yes. I know you need to check to follow protocol."

The man bustled forward, caring a small medical box. He pulled on gloves, took out a stethoscope, and dropped to his knees. Lifting the jacket, he placed the scope on the back. "No heartbeat, not surprised since his fingertips are already blue." The man shifted his weight to rest in a squatting position beside Wyn.

Mark nodded at him. "Thanks for the confirmation. We have to catalog the rest of the info before moving the body."

"Body!" Lucinda's voice rose in shrillness, which resulted in Daniel grabbing her arm, possibly to prevent the woman making a run at Mark or the paramedic. "He has a name. Wyn Lansing, my husband!" The woman yanked her arm from Daniel's to cover her face with both hands.

Donna watched Lucinda's shoulders heave as if crying. It was hard to tell with a covered face. The paramedic stood while Mark gestured for Wells to continue.

The detective gingerly approached Lucinda and held out his

hand. "Detective Mark Taber, at your service."

Daniel spoke in a sotto voice loud enough for all to hear. "He's a good guy. You can trust him."

The hands came slowly down from her face. Lucinda's lips trembled a little, but her heavy eye makeup was amazingly intact. The woman took the outstretched hand and pumped it once before dropping it as if it were a garter snake.

"Would you like to explain to me what's happening? My husband is lying in water, obviously dead. This boy," she pointed to the cop with a stabbing motion of her index finger, "decides to take snapshots like he's on a field trip or something."

"I understand your concern. We want to treat your husband's mishap with the utmost care. That includes keeping a photographic timeline."

He did that so well, with the right amount of sincerity and professionalism injected into his gravelly voice. Donna would trust him, and she already did. Lucinda sniffled, which left the men patting their pockets for non-existent tissues. Donna pulled a tissue out of her pocket. "Here."

"Thank you. Appreciate it. I talked to your brother, and he told me how you were stood up at the altar. I guess you couldn't be a floozy then. Sorry about my earlier remark."

"No problem." She gave the woman an awkward pat on the shoulder while directing a telling gaze at her brother who shrugged his shoulders. Daniel would have some reasonable explanation for dragging out her personal history to strangers when she cornered him later.

Mark squatted beside the dead man in the stream. The hem of his lightweight jacket darkened as it absorbed creek water. The purple gloves, the latex free kind, gave his hand a playful air in the gruesome tableaux. She hadn't seen him don them. It meant he expected more than an evening stroll gone awry.

Lucinda must have wondered, too. "What's with the gloves?"

Wells, who had donned a pair also, stopped talking into his shoulder-mounted radio to answer. "Standard procedure, ma'am."

Was it standard? It irked Donna that she didn't know. Mark called from his squatting position beside the body. "Got everything?"

The cop wrote something in a notebook and pocketed it before answering. "I do, now. Are you ready?"

"Almost."

The young cop had photographed the body from every angle possible, and now he was taking notes. His conscientiousness rubbed Donna the wrong way. Did first responders show up at the house of a heart attack victim and whip out the camera? No, they loaded the person or body into the ambulance. She should know since she did a two-week stint as part of the ambulance team in her early training. What she thought would be thrilling and life-changing resulted in her being bruised and battered by the erratic driving as the ambulance weaved through heavy traffic. They no longer required nurses in the ambulances.

The paramedic, whose trousers were wet to the knees, knelt on the other side of Wyn.

"Daniel," Mark called out, which resulted in her brother blocking Lucinda's view as the two men turned the body in the water.

The bruised face stared up at Donna, eyes open, the mouth partially opened in surprise as if he couldn't believe what was happening. No big surprise about that since most of her patients rebelled against their impending mortality. Why would Wyn be any different?

The medic smoothed the wet hair from Wyn's brow. "Some lacerations here from when he hit the rocks. Small stones make a big impact when hit with enough force. The blood pooled in the face since he fell head first into the water."

Lucinda stepped around Daniel and crept closer, her hand going up to her mouth as she gasped. Donna cut her eyes to Daniel's in an unspoken message. *Do something.*

The young cop inserted his body in front of Lucinda's before she made it to the water. "Ma'am, you need to wait."

"Why? It's my husband." She tried to lunge around the man who was quick to block her without using his hands. All the same, he was out of his depth. Donna knew how crazy people could be in their grief. Logical reasoning never worked. It was time for her to wade in and do what the boys couldn't.

She strolled over to Lucinda, tucked her arm into the woman's and pulled her a few steps back. "Tell me about how you and Wyn met. I always love a good love story."

The woman's eyes enlarged with confusion, but she did talk. "It was a Thursday. I always help out with Holy Rosary's Bingo Night."

That was surprising since Donna didn't take the woman for a Catholic or a bingo player. Her money would have been on a country western bar due to the big hair.

"Wyn came in with his grandmother, Doris. She's a regular player. The woman had snookered her grandson into coming, because she wanted us to meet."

She wasn't sure what surprised her more. The fact Wyn had a bingo-playing grandmother or the same woman was matchmaking for her player of a grandson. Perhaps, she wanted great-grandchildren. Lucinda continued to talk while Donna eased her away from the scene, following the stream away from the body.

Mark's voice rang out. "Call the medical examiner."

His words caused her to stumble to a halt, stopping Lucinda. The woman looked at her, possibly considering her reaction.

"Okay. I did fix the numbers so different little old ladies would win. The nuns did it, too. No one would come if the same people won all the time. Wouldn't be much of a fundraiser then."

"You're right," Donna agreed as her mind raced. The medical examiner was only called when the death was a homicide. Unlike some of the television shows, the medical examiner did not show up with the paramedics. Most cities like Legacy only had one examiner, and it was not possible or practical for that person to attend every death. Even smaller towns had to borrow MEs from bigger places, which allowed possible corruption of the scene to occur.

Her natural curiosity had her peering over her shoulder. Wells was talking into his shoulder radio while Daniel and the other paramedic crowded around the body. Mark looked up and met her gaze. His lips formed the words, *go on.*

Unfortunately, she knew what he wanted. Keep walking, keep Lucinda entertained and away from the scene. It would help them get their job done. She wasn't too sure how much she could listen to how Lucinda fixed bingo games when there was so much else she wanted to know.

"Lucinda, I know this has been a shock to you. It would be to anyone. Why don't we go back to the inn? I'll fix you some Irish coffee, and I have some fresh made cookies to go with it." She hoped she did. With any luck, Arnie had saved back some.

The woman hesitated and tried to glance back at the group. Donna weaved and bobbed, similar to a boxer, trying to block the woman's view. "You want to remember Wyn the way he looked when he entered the bingo parlor with his granny."

"But I... I should." Lucinda feinted to her left, and then went to the right to move around Donna.

Not the first time a relative of a patient tried that on her. She caught the woman's hand, interweaving the fingers. "There's nothing you can do right now. They won't let you ride in the ambulance. Later, I'll go to the morgue with you."

Good Heavens, someone needed to put a stopper in her mouth. No way she wanted to walk into a room with a bunch of stiffs. The fact they'd been refrigerated like a ham really did a number on her.

"That's kind of you." Lucinda patted her hand.

Wow, someone thought she was kind. That was a first. Maybe her efforts to be a kinder, gentler Donna were paying off. Who knew she'd have to do things like haul a grieving—observing her companion's untroubled face, she corrected herself—a widow through the woods. Now she'd have to do morgue detail unless she could find some creative way to get out of it. Could she have a phobia of dead bodies? Not too believable since she was a nurse, but Lucinda didn't know that. Then again, there was a good chance her brother had mentioned it when he gave the woman the short version of her life history in an effort to prove she had no femme fatale characteristics.

"I'm sure anyone would do as much." She murmured the words, knowing no thinking person would volunteer to assist Lucinda. Maybe a relative or close friend, of which she was neither.

"About that coffee, could I just have the whiskey and not the coffee?"

Now she had the possibility of having a drunk widow on her hands. Yay, it just kept getting better and better. "Sure. Cookies?" If she kept the woman fed and tipsy she might even forget about her promise to go to the morgue.

"Definitely cookies, the more the better. Do you have any ice cream to go with them? Chocolate syrup? Whipped cream? Crushed nuts?"

A woman after her own heart who treated emotional upsets with comfort food. "Yes to all of them."

"Good." Lucinda smoothed hair and ran a spit-dampened finger underneath each eye. "I didn't expect today to be a good day when I decided to surprise my husband and his newest squeeze. Still," she choked out the words, "I didn't expect Wyn to be dead."

Donna felt herself feeling sorry for the woman as she helped her over the rough terrain, taking her a different way to avoid the commotion at the stream. Lucinda tottered through the woods in her platform shoes, making Donna assist her up the hill, sometimes with both hands. Weren't one of the demigods punished by pushing a rock uphill? She could identify.

Once on flat land, Lucinda bent down and removed her shoes. "They're ruined anyhow. No reason to risk breaking an ankle trying to keep them on."

"You're right."

Without the shoes, Lucinda appeared smaller and more vulnerable, which made her more appealing. Of course, after she found out what a cheating dog Wyn was, there was a good chance she'd killed him. Donna took the tiniest sideway step, creating a space between the two of them. Just about the time she was working up some affection for the widow, the specter of possible homicide inserted itself. Heavens, it was hard making friends after a certain age when she was willing to consider a bingo-fixing, possible black widow as a potential lunch buddy.

Chapter Nine

A COMPACT CAR exited the inn parking lot and sped down the thoroughfare. Donna didn't have a clue who was driving. Whoever it was had a lead foot. All she'd told Arnie was to tell the guests nothing and put out cookies. Earlier today, she just wanted people to leave to be able to clean their rooms. Even though she advertised the place as a bed and breakfast, it didn't stop people asking for lunch, afternoon snacks, or fresh coffee. The first couple of visitors she had wanted to please so much she did provide them with additional nibbles and extra service, which they wrote about in their glowing review.

Donna knew the mention of a medical examiner meant Mark found something that was indicative of murder. Something obvious that didn't require toxin screens to check the blood for drugs or poisons. "Almost there." She encouraged Lucinda, who hobbled beside her. The platform shoes the woman carried may not have done her any favors, but walking the entire distance back barefoot was no treat, either.

"Good." Lucinda forced out the word. "Make my Irish Coffee a double."

"Will do," Donna responded, keeping her attention on the dog walking neighbors coming her way. The standard poodle served as their cover for gossip gathering. They'd pose a question or two as they passed. If she got Lucinda moving faster, they'd arrive at the inn sidewalk first, thus avoiding a confrontation where the foot-sore widow would say something about her cheating husband dying in the woods. No, she didn't need that.

"Hey, Lucinda. It is okay if I call you, Lucinda?"

Before the woman could reply, Donna barreled on. "Ever had a drink made especially for you?" Lucinda blinked twice, probably unsure of the question. "Well, I'm going to create a very special drink for you. After the day you've had, you deserve it."

"Amen." The woman agreed, but her pace slowed as her head swiveled, taking in the pretentious homes and their manicured lawns. "This is a nice neighborhood. I didn't pay that much attention when I strolled by with your brother. Too mad about…" Before she could elaborate, Donna hooked her arm into Lucinda's and pulled her across the neighbor's lawn. "The grass will feel better on your feet."

"Yes, I guess you're right." Lucinda smiled at the dog walkers.

Donna put up a hand in greeting, hoping they were too far away to talk. One of the men nodded, while the other looked at their feet. Walking across the grass was another neighborhood no-no. Only gardeners and lawn services personnel could do that. Children, if they ever played outside, played in the backyard.

Gossip purveyors avoided, she allowed herself to exhale. All she needed was to get the Widow Lansing up the stairs and put a stiff drink in her hand. Who knows, she might become talkative and confess all.

"Chocolate ice cream. I'd like it in my drink. I like chocolate and ice cream."

What was she talking about? Grief worked in strange ways, but Donna wasn't convinced the woman was grieving. The drink, now she'd have to make one. "Sounds great. Maybe we could call it the

Whiskey Lucinda rather like a Brandy Alexander."

"There's a brandy called Alexander? Never heard of it. Not one for those fancy drinks. I usually prefer my liquor in shot glasses."

"Okay." No surprise, there. Before they even reached the door, it swung open. Arnie, bedecked in an apron, stood there, wringing his hands.

"Donna, I tried and…" The man's woebegone face announced something hadn't gone quite right.

What else could have happened? "Tell me."

Arnie glanced down at the floor. "I'm sorry. I burnt the cookies. The second batch you put in came out fine, but when I put in the third group, Jessica came down. She wanted to know all about Wyn." Arnie colored when he realized he was speaking in front of Lucinda.

"What did you say?" Donna needed to know. Jessica knew Wyn was missing since she was the one who had notified them of his absence.

"Um, ah, I know you told me to say nothing. I really didn't, but I did mention, ah…" He angled his head in the direction of Lucinda, who was looking past Arnie, blocking the doorway, probably wondering where her whiskey was.

"Okay. Maybe you could let us in since I'm not a big fan of conversations conducted on the front step."

Arnie backed up, allowing the two of them to enter. "Any cookies left?" Donna asked, while planning how she'd keep Lucinda busy as her would-be suitor relayed the rest of his story.

"Actually, yes. A good two or three dozen since Jessica didn't eat any, just zoomed out of here."

Even though Lucinda was a couple of steps ahead, peering into each room, she stopped, cocked her head, and repeated the name.

"Jessica." She shook her head and continued on to the dining room. "I found the cookies, but where's my drink?"

"Just a minute," Donna sang out sweetly. While she jabbed an elbow into Arnie's side she hissed, "Follow me."

In the kitchen, she unlocked the cabinet that held the liquor and lifted out a whiskey bottle.

"Donna, I apologized about the cookies, but I don't think it is worth hitting the bottle over. It's not even noon."

She stopped, inhaled, *think peaceful thoughts,* and then exhaled. "It's not for me. It's for the woman in the dining room who is probably gobbling up whatever cookies are left."

The acrid burnt smell hung over the kitchen while the cookie remnants rested on the stove. "Open some windows, maybe the back door. I've got to get this stink out of here. It's not good for business." Murder wasn't good for business either, but she could only deal with one crisis at a time.

Two scoops of chocolate ice cream and two shots of whiskey should do it. She filled the shot glass again, considering adding the third, but with her luck, the woman would become a sloppy drunk, which would benefit no one. Mark would be miffed about that even though he wouldn't tell her right off. She'd have to ask him repeatedly before he'd admit his irritation.

Arnie's footsteps echoed in the back hallway where he'd opened the back door. Her fingers tightened around the third shot as she debated on pouring it back into the bottle or down the sink. Instead, she upended it into her own mouth. Not a big fan of whiskey, but it had been a rough morning.

Daniel and Mark would mention smelling alcohol on her breath. The only logical thing was to follow it with ice cream. She'd shoved a large spoonful into her mouth as Arnie walked into the room.

"Self-medicating, I see," Arnie commented.

The frozen confection melted slightly in her mouth. Thankfully, it left a cool trail, putting out the fire the whiskey had started.

"You should try it." She pushed the carton of ice cream across the counter in his direction. "It's all natural, no chemicals or artificial flavors." Donna fished out a spoon and a small dessert dish. She wrapped a paper napkin around the drink. "Help yourself. I need to get this to Lucinda, but I'll be back for a debriefing."

Her narrowed eye glance made Arnie swallow loudly. The man was already sweating, and he didn't even have a clue what had happened to Wyn.

In the dining room, Lucinda had corralled the platter of cookies and sat at the small tabletop for two with Eunice. Donna placed the drink in front of Lucinda as she blubbered into an embroidered napkin. When she had brought the delicate linens home, Maria complained they weren't practical and wouldn't hold up in the wash. Since she couldn't take them back, she defended her decision by saying she'd hand wash and iron them. Currently, the whisper thin cloth was soaking up about a pound of eye makeup and snot.

Eunice had her hand over Lucinda's and leaned over slightly to examine the glass. "Whiskey and ice cream?"

The crying stopped. Lucy's hand whipped out and grabbed the glass. A long glug emptied the glass about a quarter. The woman wiped the froth from her mouth with the back of her hand.

"It's my signature drink, Whiskey Lucinda." She held up the glass as if displaying a championship trophy. "Never had a drink named after me. Now, it might be the only thing I ever have." The woman burst into tears again.

Eunice's lips pursed, before she declared, "I could use a Whiskey Lucinda."

Great. Donna fought an eye roll. This was exactly why she didn't offer bar service. Her minimal profits would go down throats other than her own. It looked like it was going to be the type of day where she'd be making everyone drinks. As she pivoted to return to the kitchen, Eunice went with her.

A cocklebur had nothing on Eunice. At least the prickly seed never asked for drinks or high tea.

Eunice's elbow found her ribcage. "No worries about that one. She won't even know I'm not there. Too sunk into her problems."

How much did she say? Of course, Lucinda might not even realize someone killed her husband. Before she could discreetly ask, the woman pushed through the swinging door beside her.

"*Umpf.*" The two of them wedged the door open just in time to see Arnie throw back a shot of whiskey. His head pivoted enough to see the two of them wedged together like a sandwich cookie. The only things holding them together were the door frame and possibly sweat. Arnie choked hard, not too surprising since he'd been caught chugging her liquor especially after criticizing her for the same thing.

Donna wiggled her shoulders while Eunice kicked out violently, causing the two of them to tumble into the kitchen in a tangle of arms and legs. The sound of hard hacking changed to laughter. Eunice grumbled while Donna stood and offered her hand to help her up.

"Mercy! This place might be cursed." The elderly woman stood and rubbed her lower back.

Not a rumor she wanted to be spread around town. "Oh no, today isn't a typical day." At least, she hoped it wasn't and wasn't sure she could handle too many more like it. With the way her luck was running, Eunice would hit her with a lawsuit for bodily injury.

The woman boosted herself onto a stool and slapped the counter. "Where's my drink? After that tussle, I might need two."

Donna hurried over to the counter where Arnie stood. He pushed the whiskey bottle toward her as if he hadn't been imbibing. No good saying anything to the man. He probably did the same thing most of her guests would have done if left alone with an open whiskey bottle.

"All right, one Lucinda special coming up. You want one, Arnie?" The man let out a deep sigh, which she translated as *a yes*.

The three of them sat at the island sucking down their alcoholic milkshakes. The alcohol and ice cream mellowed them out, allowing them to converse easily. "I should go check on Lucinda."

Eunice swished her almost empty glass around and looked down it. Donna knew a hint when she saw one, but ignored it. Eventually, Mark would show up, and it would be better if the remaining guests were somewhat sober. "Nice of you to comfort the woman over the death of her husband since she's all broken up."

A look of amusement filled the elderly woman's eyes. Eunice shook her head and held up her glass again as if in a bar and signaling the bartender. "It's not the death of her cheating scoundrel of a spouse that has her so upset."

Ah ha, she was going to play it that way. Against her better judgement Donna reached for Eunice's glass with intentions of going heavy on the ice cream. "What's bothering her?"

"Life insurance policy. They hadn't been married all that long, and the man never got around to changing the beneficiary. Lucinda is out of everything. Wyn came from a wealthy family, according to Lucinda."

True, he was one of the privileged that received a brand new car for his sixteenth birthday while everyone else purchased old beaters by working at fast food joints.

"Did she say who the beneficiary was?"

"No." Eunice picked up her glass, gave the extra ice cream a significant look, and hid her face behind it.

If the woman knew anything else, she wasn't revealing it. The information served as a form of legal tender that she'd give out when it served her best.

Might as well check on Lucinda since she might be more forthcoming. If she knew who the beneficiary was then she'd know who benefitted from Wyn's demise. Instead of a woman crying into her whiskey-laced milkshake, Lucinda balanced the chair on two legs with her arms behind her head. Her mascara-smeared eyes reminded Donna of a silent film star, but her smile was hard and brittle, reminding Donna of a cat ready to pounce. Terri sat across from Lucinda.

What fresh hell now! The day started with a foreboding feeling and just got worse. Terri yammered on about her high school experience, extolling the virtues of being head cheerleader. Did the woman have no clue she was about five seconds from having Lucinda flying across the table?

Did Terri even know she was talking to Wyn's wife? Did she even know Wyn was dead? That would depend on the woman shutting up enough to listen to someone else, which she seldom did. A miracle happened. The woman stopped talking and looked at Donna. She pointed with one manicured finger to Lucinda's empty glass. "I'd like one of those."

Seriously. Wouldn't be surprised if Terri was Wyn's beneficiary, and Lucinda knew it. "Bar's closed. Too bad you missed out."

"What?" The outraged woman held up her hands in disbelief. "Everybody gets served, but me?"

"Nope, not everyone. Most of the guests are gone for the day. Besides being an inn, this is my home, and I can choose to offer a friend a drink. Hot and cold liquor is not part of the reunion package." She nodded to Lucinda. "Anything I can do for you?"

The brittle smile vanished as her expression softened. "Well, there's a lot I'd like done." She angled her head in Terri's direction. "But nothing you can do, though I appreciate the thought."

That should be her signal to disappear, but she didn't really want bloodshed on her rug. Something needed to be done besides throwing cold water on the two of them. Where was that reunion agenda Maria insisted on her keeping? She'd suggested the guests would appreciate it since they might forget their own. She had no interest in reunion herself, but Maria may have placed the list near the check-in table in the foyer. Donna walked backward slowly, keeping her eye on both women. Calmness settled over Lucinda, making Donna think of a storm or more likely a hurricane eye. A paperweight held down a sheaf of papers. That must be it.

She'd looked away for a second to grab the papers, which resulted in the paperweight bouncing onto the floor. The distorted sphere rolled awkwardly until it met the floor trim. Donna rushed back flipping the pages, hoping some planned event would appeal to Diva Terri. If she could get one of them out of the inn, everyone might survive to live another day.

The tiny font made reading challenging. *Science Nerds Get Together* would be held in the science lab. Couldn't expect Terri to be too into that. The basketball and football teams would convene at Kelsey's Sports Bar. There's bound to be someone Terri either knew or slept with there.

"Hey, Terri, why aren't you at the cheerleader round table. I hear they're meeting at Kelsey's Sports Bar. I bet there might even be a few football and basketball players there, too."

The woman gave her a long, disbelieving look. She wasn't accepting the bait. It would help if she used a more attractive cheese. "I imagine the women at Kelsey's will give a collective sigh since they don't have to compete with you. Good deal for them because you don't look near your age."

Before she could pile it on even more by mentioning former cheerleaders having panels sewn into their outfits to make them fit, Terri hit the stairs two at a time.

Eunice came out of the kitchen, weaving slightly. She slapped one hand against the wall to keep her balance. "Good job, almost as well as I could do. I'm feeling a little sleepy. I'm off to take a nap."

Donna watched her unsteady stroll, debating if she should help her, but the woman made it to her door. Who else did she need to monitor? Lucinda looked like the cat that just had her toy ripped away. Maybe she'd underestimated the woman. Could be she was much more solid than she originally thought, and all of this could be an act. Arnie would be her next candidate to check on.

The front door slammed open, stopping her from returning to the kitchen. Daniel entered first and gave her an unreadable look. Mark followed, his expression was easier to decipher, *resigned*. Wells looked unsure. None of the expressions boded well.

"Are all the guests here?" Mark asked, pivoting to peer in the open rooms.

The sound of high heels clattering down the stairs drew everyone's attention. Terri paused on the landing in sky high heels, a spandex skirt, and a top low enough for a doctor to do an exam without removing any clothing.

Donna would label it a dramatic pause since Terri waited until she knew she was the star and announced, "I'm late. I'm sure the other cheerleaders will be so upset. They probably have a surprise for me or something."

Keep a stoic expression. Donna held her breath, trying not to twitch and tip off Terri that there wasn't anything going on at Kelsey's. Well, nothing that involved cheerleaders. Due to the woman's inflated opinion of herself, she'd blame Donna for getting the restaurant wrong, not once considering that the other cheerleaders were more likely to build her a funeral pyre than throw her a party.

Mark moved to block the rushing woman's descent, but Donna caught his arm, shaking her head. She mouthed the words, *I'll explain later.*

There weren't a whole lot of things she could guarantee, but she'd put money on Terri returning, if not to torture the rest of them, at least for her designer luggage.

Chapter Ten

S TIFF WHITE BOWS bedecked numerous folding chairs, forming a half circle in the wedding parlor. Donna knew the arrangement was for the questioning of her guests and a possible murderer. People could decide to go stay at a popular chain motel that had pay-per-view movies with sandpaper towels. At least they wouldn't get the third degree as part of their stay.

"Mark, I don't like this. It isn't good for business."

He gestured to Officer Wells, who sat in one chair. He took the other, rocked it back on two legs, while ignoring Donna's grimace. He snapped the chair back, making the plastic groan with the motion.

Okay, they weren't the top of the line chairs. Despite her advertising the possibility of an intimate wedding, there had been no takers. Still, she didn't need the wedding chairs breaking during a murder investigation.

The last thing she needed was another murder associated with the inn. "Maybe you could tell them it was a type of mystery game."

"What a ridiculous notion." Mark rubbed his hand over the back of his neck. "Wells isn't exactly low key in his uniform, but I'm sure there's some way you can make it ordinary."

There was no great way to usher the guests in to talk to the man who'd poured them wine the night before. Eunice appeared at the door bending and flexing her legs, which was probably as close to jumping with joy as she could get. Apparently, the nap forgotten.

"Pick me!"

Pretend this is normal. "Wyn has vanished, and we're trying to get some information."

"Come on, girlie. I know Wyn's dead. Save it for some of your delicate guests like the quarreling wedding couple or the antique boys that are scooping up all the good buys in the area." Eunice grinned and pointed back to herself. "Now, I have a good eye. That's why I should be first!"

"Good argument but they asked to see Lucinda first. You can help me fix up snacks and drinks. Later, when you're *helping them,* you can grab some nibbles."

The elderly woman cocked her head before a huge smile bloomed across her face.

Not good. Even the very short time she'd known Eunice, she'd discovered whatever was good for the woman wasn't necessarily good for The Painted Lady Inn's bottom line. Might as well find out now. "What are you thinking?"

"Ah-ha, you're getting better at this. I figure with my information and help in the kitchen you should knock another day off my tab."

Normally, she'd argue the woman down, but she wasn't feeling it today. "Do you try to work off your bill at all the bed and breakfasts?"

"Nope." She added, without the least bit of embarrassment, "Most don't need my help. Lucky for you I showed up when I did. There's a lot to recommend about this place besides your neighbor across the street."

"Really?" She hadn't heard the woman say anything positive except for the food. "What else?"

"My bed's very comfy."

Yeah, my bed is very comfortable. It's a Royal Pedic, top of the line.

Eunice bobbed her head as she spoke. "I like a real mystery, too. Work that in and you'll have mystery buffs flooding the place."

All she needed was a crime spree in sleepy Legacy. "I'll keep that in mind. Go wash your hands, and I'll meet you in the kitchen."

Donna detoured to the dining room where Lucinda paged through a coffee table book of the glories of North Carolina. While she loved her state, she knew the photos were enhanced. If it kept the new widow calm, then they could insert rainbows and unicorns in every picture.

"Hey, Lucy." She went with the abbreviated name because it made them almost friends. Her hand landed briefly on the woman's shoulder. "Mark, my friend, would like to ask you some questions to figure out what happened to Wyn."

Her eyes drifted up from the book. She squinted a little in the strong light that came through the long windows. "You mean your love bunny?"

"No! Don't say that!" Donna spun around to make sure no one overheard her bizarre comment. "I'm not sure where you got that idea." Better, why did she even mention it?

"I'll admit I was all broken up about Wyn but not so much that I didn't notice the two of you had some sort of non-verbal shorthand. I certainly didn't have that with Wyn."

Donna never thought about it that way. Did it mean something other than they both tended to show up at murders? "Okay." She wasn't willing to elaborate. "I'll show you to the parlor. Then, I'll bring in some yummy snacks. Mark's a good detective. He'll get to the bottom of this."

Lucinda stood slowly and gave her a sad smile. "There you go again, talking the man up."

Had she been doing that? It was a fact, not some sort of puffery. "This way." She used her hand to gesture down the hall. Lucinda could have found the place on her own. The inn wasn't so big that she needed a tour guide, but Donna felt reluctant to leave the woman to her own devices.

"When I remodeled the place, I decided to make use of the several parlors. One's a dining room, the second and third-floor parlors I made into snack lounges. And this one is..." Donna hesitated, realizing that mentioning a wedding chapel might not be tactful. Lucinda stood in the parlor doorway. Her gaze touched on the seated men, bounced over to the fireplace with the ornate mirror over it, then on to the decorative metal arch and altar pushed to the far side of the room.

"Oh, it's a wedding chapel." Her voice carried a note of surprise.

Donna expected immediate waterworks, which was the entire reason she almost bit her tongue, trying not to mention the obvious. "Yes, it is."

"You seem like a nice person," Lucinda declared.

Nothing good ever came from a conversational volley that started like that. It was right up there with *I don't want to hurt your feelings,* and then the speaker would go on to do exactly that. What now?

Lucinda turned and gave an accusing look. "I expected better of you, a contemporary business woman. I see you too have fallen into the cultural bias."

Contemporary businesswoman. Yes, she was that as opposed to say a historical business person. *Cultural bias?* What cultural bias? Everything about the remark seemed so surreal, but considering her day, maybe it made sense.

An expansive hand wave indicating the chapel accompanied Lucinda's remark. "The entire wedding industry. Everyone has to marry to fit in. You of all people should know better since you were left at the altar."

Who was this person? Donna slid back a step. Safe to say the grieving widow had moved on to the anger stage. Anyone who had the bad taste to fall in love and marry was somehow marching to society's drum.

How did the room appear to someone who wasn't face down in love, inhaling the intoxicating fumes of romance done well? Donna squinted her eyes to view it as someone who hadn't mortgaged her home to finance it. The high windows and ceiling gave it a pleasing airy feel, but all the white decor washed out the room, especially with the sunlight streaming through the windows. The only spot of color was the seated men staring back at them.

Wells' face remained non-committal, but his upright posture radiated a certain intentness. The man exhibited anxiousness to make a good impression on Mark, or he had the murder-case jitters.

Her eyes slid over to Mark, who gave her a pitying smile. Not the kind of thing he'd trot out for an investigation. It made her curious for the briefest second. The light bulb above her head blinked on. *He'd heard.*

Humiliation raced through her faster than Jasper could grab a treat from mid-air. Despite the dog's chubby appearance, he could be fast when it came to food. The sympathetic look Mark directed at her grated.

Her nose wrinkled as she considered a killer residing in her establishment. Okay, second least favorite thing. The possibility of the newspaper getting wind of the murder and somehow connecting the inn with it took over second place, dropping the dumped-by-fiancé-tale down to third. Mark's voice interrupted her mental cataloging of bad events she didn't want to consider.

"Donna, I wouldn't mind some coffee."

Her cue to resume the innkeeper personna. *Yeah, coffee,* she turned toward the kitchen to start a fresh batch. A loud metal crash came from the kitchen along with raised voices. The left-at-the-altar story just dropped to four on her mental list. So many worse things were happening right now that made that old hurt past history. Her walk morphed into a jog as she hit the swinging door with her open hand. "What's going on now?"

Several plastic food boxes littered the island containing h'ordeuvres while the serving tray laid bottom up on the floor. The rich aroma of coffee scented the air and served as the background for an epic kitchen battle. It might even be worthy of those cooking reality shows.

Arnie's hands wrapped around the top of her 55-cup coffee urn while Eunice had a tight grip on the bottom. They both looked up at her question.

Eunice volunteered an answer first. "You told me my job was to help with coffee and snacks. I was trying to do my job. This man keeps interfering." She lifted one hand to gesture. Arnie gave the urn a twist, loosening the woman's grip on it. He backed up with a triumphant smile.

"See!" The elderly woman's eyes flared due to Arnie taking advantage of the opportunity.

No, Donna didn't *see* anything besides her West Bend Coffee Maker treated as if it were a tug of war rope. The stainless steel urn with its curving lines had style, which was one of the reasons she had bought it new. That and the fact that she hadn't run across any at the going-out-of-business restaurant and catering sale, where she'd snagged her cookware. Obviously, even people declaring bankruptcy couldn't part with their coffee urns.

Arnie's arms wrapped protectively around the urn, hugging it, and holding it close to his body. His voice carried a definite sneer. "Grandma Spendthrift was going to use the urn to make coffee for a couple of people. She's free with other people's money."

The man had a point.

Eunice, not to be outdone, fisted her hands on her hips. "You told me to help with the coffee and nibbles."

That she did without considering how Arnie might act since she had left him in charge and hadn't rescinded the order. "I did say that."

"Ha!" The woman did a fist bump and waggled her hips.

This was getting ugly. Right about now, she could use a live-in helper. At least she could have sent the potential helper in to work out things between the two. "I see someone started coffee." Not the best pacifying remark, but the smart thing would be to get the coffee and get out.

"I did," Arnie proudly asserted with a smile. "The drip coffee maker makes ten cups. I didn't think you'd need much more. Even if you did, the old coffee could be moved to a thermos while a new pot brews. It's certainly less wasteful than fixing fifty-five cups at once."

The man did have good business sense. Eunice waved her hands as if guiding a 747 down the runway.

"I wasn't going to fill the entire urn. Maybe half an urn with so many people to question.

Donna usually only brewed about twenty-five cups for the week-end crowd. It didn't look like this argument would die a natural death. She might as well get the snacks fixed. If she arranged the food, there'd be no reason for Eunice to barter work for a room discount. Donna bent down to pick up the tray when Arnie replied.

"Shows what you know. Most of the people left."

Donna's head came up fast, hitting the lip of the island. "Ow!" Pain penetrated her skull and radiated outward. Her hand went up to cover the bruised area as she carefully backed away from the island. Both Eunice and Arnie rushed to her side.

"Are you hurt?"

Arnie even abandoned his hold on the pot to examine her head. His fingers parted her hair looking for the point of impact.

The door swung open as Mark stuck his head in. "I was wondering—What's going on?"

Eunice answered before anyone could. "Donna nailed her head on the underside of the island when Arnie mentioned most of the guests had left."

The mere repetition made Donna moan. She brushed Arnie's fingers out of her hair. He reminded her of the little old men patients who always tried to cop a feel. The psychologist on staff asserted the diminished capacity of their frontal lobe explained their behavior, although she believed they knew exactly what they were doing and used their age as an excuse.

Mark grumbled, probably not for the same reason. Each weekender represented about $300 profit. Long-term guests like Marvin and Dean meant more. The reunion weekend had been a big money sucking promotion with the specialized wine and gift baskets, not to mention the expensive ad she'd taken out on the reunion website. "They all left just like that?"

Donna poured the finished coffee into an insulated thermos. Sometimes, when you didn't know what to do, it helped to resort to what was familar.

She moved around Mark who stood motionless, staring at Arnie. "What do you mean everyone left?"

The man she'd left in charge of the kitchen wilted a little under the detective's long, piercing appraisal. "Well, ah, Donna told me to say nothing."

True. She hadn't expected a murder or the need to keep her guests sequestered for questioning.

Mark's expression twisted as he sent her a questioning look. She shrugged and popped the lid off the snack boxes. The *look* didn't have the same impact on her since she knew what a marshmallow he was. Any man who responded 911 calls from children whose dogs had been hit, and then drove the injured dog to the vet wasn't exactly scary in her book.

The possible evaporation of her opportunity to lessen her expenses sent Eunice rushing to the island. She grabbed the tray and pulled it out of Donna's reach. "Here, let me do that."

Great. You give people a little responsibility and they go crazy with it. She snatched the tray back from Eunice with a satisfying tug. The woman's crestfallen face made her add, "We'll both do it."

Arnie's pleading expression reminded her a little of Jasper when she took him to the vet or rather when he finally realized where they were going. She should say something. "Oh, I never told him to keep the people from leaving. There wasn't a reason to do that."

Arnie shook his head so hard he resembled a bobble head doll. "That's right. I didn't tell anyone Wyn was dead."

The nibbles and coffee were ready. All she needed were cups, sugar, creamer, and spoons. Maybe she should make hot water for tea. Undecided, she opened the tea box to decide what tea went best with police interrogation. Possibly peppermint, if a person felt an upset stomach about the thought of murder.

"Donna?" Mark spoke, somehow making her name into a question.

Yeah, she knew he blamed her for that information leak. "I didn't tell him, although, Lucinda did mention it." She cut her eyes to Eunice who was standing nearby.

"I saw that. Go ahead and try to pin it on me after you accused Arnie of killing that nice man."

Mark's eyebrows shot up farther than she'd ever seen them go. Now, Eunice refers to Wyn as that *nice man* where before she labeled him a self-important peacock. Rushing Lucinda back had rattled her some. Even though she had made small talk the entire way back, her mind was full of calculations of what another murder would do to her hotel's bottom line. Somehow, she'd actually forgotten she'd questioned Arnie.

Not a whole lot to say to that. She picked up the tray, carried it to the door and backed into it. When in doubt, leave. The door swung back and forth rapidly which had the effect of making Arnie's remark soft, then loud, then soft again.

"I told *Donna* I *didn't* kill *Wyn*."

Eunice now knew, which was the same as the entire world knowing.

The only way to keep her quiet would be to lock her in the basement. Since the house wasn't soundproof all the hammering and yelling would result in rumors that the place was haunted by a belligerent ghost. Grumpy ghosts seldom attracted paying guests. Then there was the possibility of the woman emptying her limited wine cellar, too. Herman might like to squire the opinionated female around if she asked nicely and footed the bill. At the rate the inn sucked up money, she'd still be a nurse into her nineties. The only nurse older than her geriatric patients. Her lips twisted in disgust at the image. Not happening. The best way to make it not happen was to clear the inn of any connection to the murder.

Wells and Lucinda had their heads close together. Donna called on her stealth skills from Girl Scouts to slip up to the couple. The skills she learned as a young scout weren't the hunting type, but rather slipping up to doors and pretending to hawk cookies. At the time, she didn't like the idea of selling cookies. Here she was forty plus years later, selling cookies with an overnight stay included, along with breakfast.

Wells angled his head to Lucinda. "Who do you like in the World Series?"

The woman put a finger to a nose as if considering. "The National League usually has a good team, but not this year."

Donna's biceps ached under the weight of the heavy tray, but she was unsure if she should say anything. This might be a new procedure to withdraw information without seeming to. What did it mean that the National League didn't have a good team? Should she be able to read something into this?

Mark's footsteps sounded as he entered the room. "Donna, what are you doing?"

Eavesdropping wouldn't work as a reply. "I didn't want to interrupt."

The two looked up, and Wells even smiled, when he caught site of the coffee thermos.

Lucinda pointed to the thermos. "Could I have my coffee with whiskey like my drink?"

Mark cleared his throat behind her. *So much for their little secret.*

"That was just for shock. You're better now."

The woman looked disappointed but nodded in agreement. "Okay. Remember every time you make that drink, you have to call it the Whiskey Lucinda."

Donna placed the tray of goodies on a nearby drum table. Each coffee cup had a saucer. She placed a spoon by it, and then added the folded napkin. "I will," Donna sang out her reply, not looking up and meeting Mark's eyes.

No need to see what they might say. She already knew. It would be something about compromising a case. In the end, she'd have to find a clue to nail the killer to prove her worth. After all, she was essential to solving the murder that happened in her upstairs parlor last year. As inn owner and part time maid, it gave her the right to search the guest rooms while cleaning them, of course.

Chapter Eleven

DONNA GRABBED THE guest roster with plans of searching each room under the guise of cleaning. How cool was that? On most detective shows, they had to jump through hoops to do undercover work while she could get into the rooms with her own key. What she needed to know was who had left and when they'd be back. Arnie could probably tell her.

Back in the kitchen, she discovered Arnie and Eunice seated at the island, sipping coffee and nibbling on praline cheesecake she knew had been in the freezer.

"Enjoying yourselves?" Arnie looked up and blessed her with a devoted look. The man had a lot in common with his clients, or make that his clients' pets.

"I am. I've never been a part of an actual murder case. It's like I'm in a movie of the week."

Eunice added, "I'd like Kate Winslet to play me."

Donna couldn't fight off an eye roll.

The back door opened, bringing indoors the scent of autumn and Daniel. "Hey. Came by to see how things were here."

Both Arnie and Eunice waved and chirped their hellos. Everyone liked her brother. Daniel chatted with the two while she searched the junk drawer for a pen. The drawer usually held chopsticks and promotional key rings, but never anything useful, like a pen.

Arnie confided to Daniel about being part of an actual murder case. "I might be on television." His brow furrowed as he added, "I could mention my pet butler service."

At least, her brother didn't ask how Arnie knew about Wyn's death. Yeah, he probably knew she was the culprit. Daniel poured himself a cup of coffee and hooked a stool with his foot. "Arnie," he nodded in the man's direction, "don't set your heart on a book deal. If you saw where and how we found him, it's understandable why he's dead. Wyn probably blundered into a drug deal going down."

Her earlier enthusiasm about searching rooms died a bit. The searching would involve cleaning. Unfortunately, some people did expect it, the cleaning, not the searching. "Got a pen, Danny Boy?"

Their great uncle Matthew used to love to call Daniel, Danny Boy, then would attempt to sing the Irish ballad if he was drinking heavily. Often he couldn't remember Donna's name until Daniel suggested calling her, Donna Girl.

"Here ya go." He pulled a pen from his pocket.

Donna scribbled down the names and room numbers. Eunice peeked over her shoulder.

"What's this? Possible murderers? Where's my name?"

It was, only she didn't want to admit to it. Eunice sounded disappointed about not making the list. The woman was annoying, rather like a fluffy dog that barked continually. "It's my room cleaning list. By the way, where's Jasper?" It had been a hectic morning, and she remembered seeing the dog on his way up the stairs to greet his newest fan and treat giver.

"Babbles," Arnie muttered, then placed the coffee cup to his lips.

Donna stared at the man who made no gulping actions. He wasn't drinking. The man used the cup as a shield. "The Babbles. May I ask who told George and Helen they could take my dog?"

Eunice made a shushing sound. "Simmer down. Don't be so

hard on your beau. He means well, even if he's the crap king."

Arnie put his cup down to reply. "I prefer Dog Butler Million-aire."

This was getting her nowhere. "I don't care if you prefer the Duke of Dog Butlery. I just want to know where my dog is." When life made awkward turns, she depended on ordinary things to regain her balance. Jasper was one of those things.

Daniel reached for her hand and squeezed it. "No one stole your dog. He's not even a purebred, and he has toxic farts." He turned to Arnie. "Did you see them take Jasper?"

"No, I didn't, but Eunice did."

The woman beamed as all eyes turned to her. "It had to be after you left. I was out taking my morning constitutional. I try to walk for twenty minutes for my health. I saw the Babbles leaving. Jasper was outside. I'm not sure if he was already outside or if they lured him out. Anyhow, he hopped into their car."

"Et tu, Jasper?" Donna knew her pooch could be had for a dog treat and a car ride. "What would you call that?"

Daniel shrugged his shoulders. "Dog lovers. They'll be back. I thought Maria mentioned them as the arguing wedding guests." Her brother colored slightly, probably realizing he talked about guests in front of other guests. It didn't take a rocket science degree to figure out how they gossiped about the guests.

A number one went by the Babbles name. She'd start with them first. Didn't think they were murderers, but hadn't thought they were dognappers, either. The least she could do was make sure their bags were still here. Luggage wasn't cheap, so most people wouldn't leave it behind.

Eunice agreed. "I wouldn't be surprised if the husband agreed to take Jasper just to keep his wife in a good mood. From what I heard last night, the wedding might be one of those new age celebrations where dogs are invited."

The wife did use Jasper as a dose of four-legged tranquilizer. Donna's earlier anxiety lessened, at least about her dog. He'd come back a little fuller and tired. Her pen hovered over Wyn's room number. His would be the one police taped off. Goodness, she hoped not. Bright orange or yellow police tape never enhanced any décor. "Did Jessica really leave?"

"It looked like it to me. I was in the dining room putting out the cookies. She tiptoed down the stairs with her bag, went out the side door, got in her car, and took off as if going to a fire. I don't really expect her back with Wyn's real wife here. Sounds suspicious to me. I'll make a point of telling Mark."

Donna scribbled the information on a piece of paper to hand off. Only it wasn't all that much since she didn't know Jessica's last name or even if Jessica was her real name. Since everything was registered in Wyn's name, she had little information to share, besides the woman departing in a manner similar to a cat burglar.

She scratched out the number one by the Babbles name and replaced it with a two. "Well, I got to get to work." She ducked into the hall, grabbed her cleaning caddy and an empty clothes basket she'd fill with the dirty linen. Each floor had their own linen closet, which helped with clean towels and changing beds. On second thought, she ducked into the laundry room, rifled through her medical kit for some latex gloves.

The last thing she needed was her fingerprints everywhere. Maybe she shouldn't clean the place. A forensic technician could show up and take DNA samples from the beard stubble in the bathroom sink or skin scales on the sheets. A look-see is all she'd need to determine the nature of Wyn and Jessica's relationship, then onto the Babbles' room if only to see if their luggage was still there.

Eunice's failure to volunteer helped support her theory that the woman didn't want to do actual work. She couldn't be much of a sleuth if she passed on a chance to nib through people's stuff.

Donna called on her stealth skills as she climbed to the third floor. It wouldn't take Mark long to realize she'd gone through each room, but it was her job. The third floor had the most bedrooms because it didn't have the extra storage room the second floor did, although it may have been a nursery or a servant room originally.

The Babbles were out. Jessica had left, as did Wyn, in a matter of speaking. Only the Christmas salesman and Lorena who managed to look elegant even while complaining about being dead tired remained. She hadn't showed up at breakfast or at the wine tasting last night. It almost made Donna wonder if she was even in her room.

The door to C1 opened, and her first arrival, Lorena, stood there. The quiet woman oozed elegance in a slim short dress paired with matching navy pumps and clutch. She blinked as if surprised to see Donna on the landing. Birds chirped outside the window. A non-bird lover might find the third floor overwhelming since trees surrounded the inn and most built their nests around the third floor and upward. "Good Morning. Sorry you missed breakfast. Would you like me to get you a snack?"

The woman gave her a cool smile. "No, thank you. I'm meeting a friend, and we're going out to lunch, then we'll have our nails done and possibly take in a movie."

"Sounds like a great day. Have fun." She watched the woman walk down the stairs with a pang of envy. The woman had it all, classic beauty, good manners, and self-control. Most people would run down the stairs just for the free food or they'd rationalize it as food they'd purchased, which was true.

Maybe she should have mentioned Mark questioning the guests. It would do no good to talk to her since she never saw her. If he wanted to detain her, then he'd need to do it on his own.

All clear, unless Jeff Ferguson was squirreled away, making Christmas toys to sell. He could have tiny little hammers and saws in his suitcase. It didn't matter if he did as long as he kept the room tidy and the floor scratch-free.

Gloves on, she opened Wyn's door. No ominous creak, no bloodstains or noxious odor. Her eyes traveled over the familiar surfaces looking for anything out of place. Only one side of the bed was mussed and one head print marked a single pillow where a solitary person slept last night. Her money would be on Jessica as the sleeper.

No luggage left behind, and the two of them had only brought one suitcase. In the bathroom, she sniffed the air. Nothing, except the scent of the spicy potpourri in a crystal bowl. A man, especially one consumed with his appearance, would have used a variety of grooming products, each with its own distinctive smell. Nothing, not even a hint of a female cologne to suggest anyone had been here. She pulled the shower curtain aside to find the tub perfectly dry. Even the cake of French milled soap hadn't been opened. *Strange.*

A glance at the toilet paper revealed that the triangle fold she always put on the end of the tissue was gone, which meant at least that had been used. More likely by Jessica than Wyn although she couldn't be sure. No toothpaste scum or beard stubble in the sink or someone went to the trouble to clean it up. Most people weren't that considerate. It would be especially hard to trace someone with no last name. Donna tried hard to bring Jessica's face into focus. Most of the time the woman had bent at the waist, allowing her straight brown hair to hide her face as she pulled the suitcase into the foyer. Jessica had skipped the wine tasting, even though Wyn hadn't. This morning was the only time she'd glimpsed her rather ordinary face, which had been pale.

Donna glanced at the mirror, which was also spotless. No face washing or teeth brushing spatter, which meant everything had been cleaned. No one was that neat. What was Jessica's deal with Wyn? The single side of the bed didn't indicate any unbridled passion. Why did she even come if the man had intended to hook up with an old girlfriend? The mirror didn't give her any hints. Jessica, with an urge to wipe away any evidence of ever being there, left none, except for the bed. Even that was suspect. It could have been staged for someone to feel sorry for the betrayed wife, a pretense that fell apart when Lucinda showed up.

"Discover anything?" Mark called from the bedroom.

That was a surprise. She expected a lecture about contaminating a crime scene. "Not in the bathroom. Never used the shower. I think the sink is cleaner than it was when they checked in." She held up her hands to display the gloves.

"Good deal." He sighed deeply. "Would you listen if I told you not to go snooping into things that aren't your business?"

Did he really expect an answer? They'd had the same discussion a half dozen times when Mark had investigated the unknown dead man previously found on her third floor. Peculiar that they'd be on the third floor again and there'd been another dead man. She drew up her mouth and pretended to consider the matter, rolling her eyes upward to complete the pretense. After a quick couple of seconds, she shook her head.

"That's what I thought." His hand ruffled his salt and pepper hair. "I'll get Wells up here to take some photos."

"What about our forensic unit?" Donna asked, wondering if the mysterious Jessica had left a clue behind.

"Again? You know Legacy doesn't have a forensic unit. I can dust for prints. I can send off the sheets for analysis."

The sheets that would be a loss of eighty dollars. If she had known the outcome, she'd have put the cheap bargain sheets on the bed. "Okay. Do what you need to do."

Mark snorted as he lowered himself to the floor and looked under the bed. "I commend you on your housekeeping and the lack of dust bunnies."

It had never occurred to her that people would be looking underneath her beds. She knelt beside Mark trying to see what he saw from his angle. A whole lot of nothing, besides a clean stretch of wooden floor. Green paper curled around a bed frame foot. "What's that?"

"Could be evidence." Mark straightened, pulled a plastic evidence bag from his coat and opened it. "I want you to reach for it with this." A pair of blue plastic tweezers appeared in his hand.

Donna took them and lay on the floor where she last saw the mysterious paper. "Lift up the coverlet to give me some light."

What was the paper? A love note? Perhaps instructions on how to get rid of Lucinda? A price tag from a high-end store? The blue tweezers closed on the paper. As she drew it out, she realized it was money.

Mark held out the bag, and she carefully dropped the bill into it.

"It's just money." It would be money she wouldn't see again since it would now be classified as evidence.

"Hmm, I wouldn't say that." He held the plastic bag up to the sun streaming through the window.

"How much? I might as well know how much I'm not getting."

"Come look."

The idea depressed her, but she might as well. A teaching moment where he tried to enlighten her that actual police work wasn't anything like television. The clues were minuscule, few, and more likely an informant ratting someone out tied up a case.

Mark held the plastic bag up. "What do you see?"

She saw a five-hundred dollar bill with a crease down the middle. "Is that McKinley on it?"

"It is. Notice anything else?"

Trick question. It looked authentic, although she'd never had that big of a bill in her hand. She peered at the small print on the paper. "It was printed this year at the Denver mint."

"Exactly. One-hundred dollar bills are the largest bills printed now."

No wonder Jessica's room was so spotless, considering what a lovely job she did with the money. "Does that mean she and Wyn are counterfeiters?"

"It's hard to say without talking to them. Could be their job was to spread the money around. Legacy is a likely spot, but most retailers are wary of anything larger than a fifty. Could be a payoff for something. The money's destination could be out of the country. Then again, they could be fools who didn't know five-hundred dollar bills aren't in circulation."

"Hey! I take offense at the *fool* label." It surprised her that she didn't know. After all, shouldn't she be aware of the currency she used every day?

Mark pocketed the bill. "What if someone paid you with counterfeit five hundred dollar bills?"

Another trick question or maybe it was a trick answer. "Maria takes a credit card number and runs it to make sure it is legitimate before booking the room. We usually charge one night to hold the room. Although we can reverse the charges if someone wants to pay in cash. I mainly do the one night charge to prevent the no-shows. It usually works."

"Donna, repeat what you just said."

Seriously, the man had ignored her. "Maria takes a credit card number and…" She stumbled to a halt. "The credit card number?"

"We need that number. It's possible he used someone else's. Still, I'm sure whatever reason Wyn had for showing up here, he didn't expect to end up dead, which means it's a legitimate card. It might even belong to the mysterious Jessica."

Donna drifted to the window and observed the tree leaves starting to change color. What was going through Wyn's mind when he stood in the same place? Was he thinking about a suitcase of money? She doubted it. Whatever transaction he had going on, he'd probably put Jessica in charge of it since he was too busy handling his various love interests. No wonder the woman was holding onto the suitcase.

The wood floor creaked slightly as Mark stepped behind her.

"I think the reunion was a cover."

It made sense. "It had to be what he told Lucinda since she followed him here."

"Agreed. Maybe he met his contact in the woods. Someone he was supposed to hand the money off to. Whoever it was shot him and took the money."

It sounded probable, but something bothered her about it. Wyn could have arranged to meet someone near the woods, but after he left the neighborhood, the streetlights would be rare. Last night's moon was a fingernail moon giving very little illumination to the path.

"He could have picked your inn because of the closeness to the drop point."

"Well, that means the ad I took out was a waste. Terri made a point of mentioning Wyn told her to stay here since he was. She acted very put out that she had to stay here. Do you think she was involved in a counterfeit scheme?" Part of her wanted the vindictive woman carted away in handcuffs. Dozens of people had to have felt the wrath of the woman or had her stiletto planted on their soft skin as she climbed over them to get where she wanted. A satisfied sigh escaped her lips.

"I'm afraid to ask what you're thinking about."

The truth would only make her look petty. "Hmm, as much as I might want Terri involved, she was only here for a hookup. It gave her a brief moment of reliving her high school days. I'd bet Wyn spent the first part of the night in her room."

Even without turning around, she knew Mark was running his hand over his face the way he usually did when he thought. The beginning beard stubble rasped under his fingertips. He cleared his throat, meaning he'd come to a conclusion. It was scary how well she knew him.

"I imagine you have a room to clean."

No reason for him to mention whose room. From her spot at the window, she saw movement in the parking lot. "Someone is leaving."

Mark bumped her shoulder as he jockeyed for position beside her. "Who is it?"

"A man with a beard heading toward a panel van emblazoned with a Christmas Tree. It must be Jeff Ferguson. Strange, I didn't see him on the steps or in the parlor. He must have left after I entered this room."

"He could have left to avoid questioning about his whereabouts."

In novels and sometimes television mysteries, the least likely person was the guilty one, which made her St. Nick clone a real contender. "Come on, I think you could safely mark him off your list. If they had any exchanges to make they could have done it in the parking lot."

They both watched the van drive away. It was a Saturday, not a great day to be showing off his seasonal merchandise.

"Donna, you may not be aware of it, but you have very suspicious neighbors who watch the inn like a hawk, especially your litigious neighbor down the street."

His comment surprised a laugh out of her. "Har! Har! The woman who tried to sue me because the workers made too much noise putting in the parking lot. It was finished before the judge even read the complaint, which made it a moot point."

"Could be," Mark said, as he eyed the quickly disappearing van, "they planned a drop here, not knowing how busy your neighborhood was."

If a person hadn't been in Legacy for over twenty or more years, they'd be shocked at how the houses had been returned to their former glory. Although current homeowners tended to imply the older homes had been in the family for generations instead of bought cheap and refurbished. It made her wonder why they objected to her presence when she did the same thing.

"True. There's always someone out. The neighbors have more of an involuntary watch. If there were criminal types lurking about, they'd notice."

Instead of answering, he stood at the window, staring at nothing as much as his inner landscape. The silence deepened as Donna wondered what he could be thinking. A solitary bird trill broke the silence. Mark tipped his head slightly.

"I thought you had a room to clean."

Chapter Twelve

DONNA LOADED UP on fresh towels before heading off to Terri's room. Her chin held the fluffy towels in place as she unlocked the door. The expensive fabric softener tantalized her nose with a pleasant fragrance on a day that had few perks so far. The woman was probably the type who used every towel in the bathroom for a single bath, leaving a wet heap for the help to pick up. Even though it was her job to clean the rooms, she gave a furtive glance behind her as the door swung open. No one was on the landing or coming up the stairs. Mark must still be in Wyn's room.

The questioning must be over since most of the guests had left. They couldn't tell people why they wanted to question them without them possibly clamming up. A chair propped the door slightly open to let the guest know the room was in the cleaning process. This time, she wanted advance warning if Terri returned. She slipped off her shoes to be quiet in case someone was on the second floor. Outside of Eunice and Arnie, everyone had left, but people could come back. She placed the cleaning caddy on the table and withdrew her phone. Technically, Mark couldn't enter the room without probable cause. Donna would snap a few shots to see if there was enough for a search warrant.

The trail of clothing started in the narrow hallway: stiletto, and then another, a man's shirt, then a belt. It wasn't hard to deduce that Terri hadn't been alone for at least part of last night. It had to be

Wyn. She'd checked the front door at ten, but someone could have locked the door after him.

A quick peek into the bathroom revealed spilled shampoo, a truckload of beauty products scattered across the counter. No surprise there. It might explain why Wyn's bathroom was so clean. She aimed the camera for another photo. Technically, she'd have to clean the room. Couldn't call it a crime scene and leave it a mess.

Donna knew she'd find evidence of a tryst with a married man. Most would have tried to hide it. With Terri, it was a badge of honor. *Look, I can steal someone's husband.* Why she thought hooking up with a player was a lofty goal boggled the mind.

Wait, she glanced at the shirt again. Did Wyn have that shirt on at the reception? The striped shirt wasn't the gold one he wore downstairs. Her lips twisted as she pictured the man face down in the stream. She couldn't see his shirt from her angle. If it were the gold striped shirt, then he went from the reception to meet someone, which would have made it easy to slip out the door with the party breaking up and her carrying out the platters.

No one would have been monitoring the front door. She'd have to ask Mark what Wyn had on when they found him. Donna steeled herself for whatever damage they may have done to the bedroom in their attempt to relive their youth. The rumpled white comforter and the two pillows bore head prints, indicating that Terri had company. Even though Donna assumed Wyn was her guest, she couldn't prove it. At best, it was circumstantial evidence.

For all she knew, she could have been entertaining Mr. Babble, which would have explained his wife's attitude. Donna moved slowly around the room, taking a snapshot every few feet. Even if she found a box of counterfeit money, she couldn't touch it. The best she could do was tell Mark, who would get a search warrant, which could be tricky on a weekend. By that time, the money could vanish.

It's no wonder a third of the murders go unsolved in the United States. Donna glared at the bed, knowing she'd have to change the linen. Good thing she kept her gloves on. Would Mark need the sheets for a DNA recovery? If so, he wouldn't have to obtain them illegally. They were her sheets to do with as she pleased.

Still, she couldn't take a chance on them being mixed up with the other linens. A garbage bag would be her oversized specimen bag. She'd do the same with towels. The loss of bed linens and a towel set would be a small hardship if it helped catch a killer. After extensive forensic tests, the material would prove that Wyn was in the room, which was a no-brainer. Her fingers wrapped around a corner of the sheet and pulled it from the mattress. Her mind wandered as she tried to remember why there was such a drop in solving murders.

It was harder to charge a suspect, for one thing. It used to be an eyewitness was enough, but eventually, the majority of lawyers and more than a handful of legislators realized that sometimes the credibility of a witness could be dubious. It reminded her of a movie courtroom scene where the lawyer pointed out the woman who claimed to see the suspect at night from her window when the streetlight had been broken, which wasn't possible.

There was always a chain of evidence to follow, no matter how many people announced they wanted to kill someone. The throw-away phrase *I could kill you* was probably uttered every day about the same number of times as *Do you want fries with that?*

There were no tears in the sheets, which proved their reunion wasn't as vigorous as implied by Terri's sly smile this morning. Unfortunately, trying to obtain evidence from them might not leave them in such great condition either. She might never see them again.

The tied garbage bag sat by the door.

Thank goodness her comforter wasn't a victim of shared passion since replacing the item would be pricey. Even purchased at a hundred and twenty dollars on clearance, money she didn't have to replace it. No way could she find another clearance sale that good.

A car door closing propelled her to the window. The window faced west, which gave her a view of the house next door, the tree outside of the window, and the dog walkers. No good. She exited the room for a third-floor parlor window. There was a navy sedan with a man standing beside it. Couldn't be Father Christmas since he had left in a white panel van, which was the preferred vehicle of kidnappers and serial killers according to television. A dog jumped out of the car, stopped, and looked up. Jasper, of course. He must have felt her mental condemnation at going with strangers for the price of a dog treat, but her dog was home, which was a plus. The Babbles were back, which meant she'd have to bypass their room until they left again.

Cleaning while the guests kicked back in the room made her uncomfortable. Time to get Terri's done. She might be able to finish Ferguson's room too before his return. He might be the accomplice, then again the Babbles could be only pretending to be wedding guests.

Back in the room with fresh linens, she changed the bed. She ran a dusting rag over the bedside table where a wilted rose and card sat. She flipped the card open.

Terri,

You were always the best thing in my life.

Wyn

Phone out, she snapped a photo of the open card. Not exactly proof positive Wyn had been there, but even for Terri, it would have been crass to leave the note visible when entertaining someone else. It demonstrated a sweetness she hadn't expected from the man. Dropping to her knees, she peered under the bed. No counterfeit money, one thong, and one shoe that she didn't feel like retrieving. She'd rather Terri downgrade her on cleanliness as opposed to picking up used underwear. Almost done with the bedroom, then on to the bathroom.

Twenty minutes later, she moved into Ferguson's room with misgivings about how easy she'd thought running a B and B would be. Thank goodness she'd never given in to her moment of insanity and offered lunch.

A strong cinnamon smell greeted her when she opened C3. A hint of pine rested under the strong spice. Pewter Christmas tree music boxes, crystal angels, and international Santas from around the world crowded every available surface. Some Santas wore the traditional red suit, a few green, one entirely in animal fur, and another in blue and white. It didn't look like the room of a potential felon, but rather like a Christmas novelty shop. No dusting since it would mean moving all the items from the surfaces.

The bed was made up and the bathroom tidy. She wasn't sure about Mark's opinion, but the man had already impressed her with his neatness. Surely, someone so clean had to be innocent or very clever.

"Are you done yet?"

Mark's voice startled her, causing a small, guilty jump. She gave the room a last satisfied study before she walked to the door.

"You gave me a scare. I'm done with this room." She carried the wet towel and cleaning caddy out to the passageway that separated the rooms from the parlor.

The towel landed in a waiting clothes basket. She checked the room off her list. "Any other rooms you consider a priority?"

Daniel's laughter below meant he was keeping the Babbles entertained. Her brother's gift of small talk worked in her favor, especially now.

Mark's hands went to his temples as he massaged them, a sign of a headache coming on. "Wish I knew. Lucinda wasn't a font of information. Eunice, on the other hand, had lots of info."

"That's good, right." Too bad the woman chose not to share the same information with her.

He gave a small snort that hovered between a laugh and expulsion of breath. By now, she realized it was his version of *seriously?*

"Not buying it?" Eunice thrived on attention. Maybe she lived alone, and this outing acted on her rather like catnip did on a feline. Perhaps she was a little crazy with the attention, elaborating on tales and such.

His hands dropped from his temples, and he sighed deeply. "Wish I knew what to believe. Ten percent of what she says could be true. The problem is figuring out what ten percent."

"Herman could help." The idea of having the man take Eunice out returned with the added possibility of information extraction.

His hand lightly touched her arm as a warning tone entered his voice. "Donna, don't even consider it. It doesn't take a village to solve a crime. It would just mess up the evidence."

As much as she hated to admit it, the man had a point. "All right, still it couldn't hurt if Herman took her out."

His lips twisted as he regarded her the way one might regard a cup of arsenic-laced purple Kool-Aid. "Only if it is of his own free will. No bribing the man with a lifetime of macadamia chocolate chip cookies."

Herman preferred her blonde brownies. "Of course not. What's the hardest thing about solving crimes?"

He gave her a long look that questioned her intentions. "Besides blocking all the help amateur sleuths try to give me?"

Was that a jab at her? "Who else could have taken the photos?"

"You got me there. No one else legally. As for your initial question, I think our current culture of not being a snitch prevents cases reaching a successful conclusion. When a crime occurs, someone knows about it. There is no perfect crime. Could be the perp drank too much and bragged about the felony in a bar. A patron or bartender could call, but they don't."

"Why? If I heard someone commenting on a murder, I'd call."

Mark's fingers rubbed the bridge of his nose as he spoke. "I've asked myself that a hundred times or more during an active case. The first is retribution. The accessories fear the criminal more than they do the legal system. The killer is up close, personal, and living in their zip code. Besides, they already know what he can and will do. Not everyone is like you and trusts the police. Instead, the police serve as their personal bogeyman, especially if they already have a warrant. Why take a chance of telling the police, ending up in jail, or practically guaranteeing a sudden demise?"

"When you put it that way, I'm surprised you solve any crimes."

Mark's rough laugh filled the room. "If ever I feel like I'm getting too big for my britches, I'll come to you to be brought down a notch or two. All the same, criminals are not the masterminds television would have you believe. They leave behind a multitude of clues. Every now and then, we even get help from concerned citizens." A brief smile illuminated his face.

It made her grin in response. "Keep in mind, this concerned citizen has a major investment in learning the identity of the killer.

Could you not mention to the press that Wyn was staying here?"

"It would be best. The killer would possibly know. At this point, there isn't much to tell, anyway." He held one finger. "I have a very special job that only you can do."

Did he want to sneak into someone's room? Her initial plan was to clean Dean and Marvin's room while she was on the third floor, but she could change room order if needed. "Go on."

The detective shook his head. The crows' feet gathering at his eyes told of his not so hidden amusement. He'd probably tell her to go out and have a great day or something equally silly.

Donna continued, "I will. Tell me."

"Glad you agreed." He glanced down at his feet before he met her eyes. "Keep Eunice from talking, especially to the press."

That's all he wanted her to do. "It would be easier to keep the sun from coming up. How do you suggest I manage that?"

His hand went up to rub against his chin again. "Hmm, I don't know. Keep her busy here. Don't let her out of your sight. Maybe she could help you."

"Ha! You didn't read her well them. The woman doesn't want to do actual work. She only wants to give the appearance of helping. Besides, having her help would negate the guest's confidentiality. I'd like to think none of my guests are killers and some will be return guests if I treat them right. Having Eunice paw through their personal items would not rate up there with good customer service."

"Okay, maybe you can think of something. I need to get back to the station and assist Wells. Can you get me the credit card number before I go?"

"Of course." She left her caddy in the parlor but picked up the garbage bag with the soiled sheets. Donna lowered her voice and spoke in what she considered her spy voice that sounded similar to a

1-900-sex operator. "I think you should be able to get some DNA off this. Sheets, you know." She shook the garbage bag.

He took the sack. "Okay." He proceeded to talk in a normal tone of voice. "It wasn't a secret that Terri and Wyn had something going on. We could get as many as four witnesses to agree to that, including you."

When he put it that way, it sounded as if she were sacrificing her sheets for no reason. "Give me the bag back then. I'll wash the sheets in hot water, and they'll be good."

She reached for the bag that Mark moved out of reach. "There might be something else useful on the sheets."

They continued down the stairs without talking. When they reached the kitchen, Donna went to the cabinet and pulled out the laptop.

"Unique hiding place."

"I have to hide it. I found a guest on it when I first opened. Guests tend to think B and B is code for I can use, eat, or drink anything I want. In a hotel, they'd accept one room. Here, they think the entire house is their domain. I'm considering locking my pantry, too, after a pound of marshmallows and a jar of peanut butter went missing."

"I see your point. Mind if I help myself to more coffee?"

Donna watched as the hourglass icon informed her it was working, but not fast enough in her opinion. "Sure, but you'll have to get it from the front parlor where you were."

Mark walked out the swinging door, grumbling to himself. "Doubt there'll be any left."

She suppressed the temptation to tell him beggars couldn't be choosy. The desktop screen flickered on. She'd moved on to the bookkeeping software by the time Mark returned.

"Any coffee?"

That man held out his cup that had about a tablespoon of brown liquid. His forlorn expression made her giggle. "I'll make some more. You might need it since we don't have the full number of Wyn's credit card. Just the last four digits. I know when it expires, the bank, and even the security code." She turned the computer so Mark could look at it while she started the coffee.

"Have you charged him yet?"

No, she hadn't. "I usually don't charge until a person leaves. That way they only have one charge."

Mark perused the screen and tapped on a few keys while she poured water into the coffee maker. The machine gave a few steamy coughs, then settled into the transformation process of changing ordinary tap water and ground coffee beans into a life-giving elixir.

"Coffee should be ready in about five minutes." She wondered about a snack. Breakfast seemed like forever and a day ago. The kitchen clock showed it had only been a little less than three hours. "Did you eat anything I put out earlier?"

"Afraid I might get my hand bit off, the way your guests were going at the snacks." He gave her a sheepish grin that made her wonder if he embellished scenarios as much as Eunice did.

"Indonesian chicken satay with sauce?"

His grin grew even wider, making her wonder if the man had hoped she'd offer him something to eat.

"Sounds like heaven to me."

No matter what she offered him, he always seemed appreciative. "I'll reheat it in the microwave if you don't mind."

"Of course not." His slim notebook was out as he copied information from the screen.

"I could have printed it."

"Yeah, but I'm a creature of habit. This is what I do. Give me a half-dozen printed pages and I'd lose them."

Yep, she had to concur on the *creature of habit* part. The notebook was as much a part of him as his graying hair. "Think you can trace the card?"

"Not sure, this is where some type of forensic accountant would come in handy, but I have an idea."

She was not too thrilled with his last idea that had Eunice and her joined at the hip. She wasn't sure she would like this one either. "Where's Eunice?"

"She told me she was going to take a nap." Mark glanced over at the coffee maker, liking what he saw. He carried his cup over and poured himself a cup.

Some people might resent Mark making himself at home, but Donna preferred it to expecting hand and foot service as the guests did.

"You want some?"

At her nod, he pulled a clean cup out of the cabinet, filled it, and carried it to the table. She gave him a grateful smile before sipping the hot brew. Three sips later she felt restored enough to ask the dreaded question. "What do you want me to do?"

"A little thing really. Charge Wyn's card for the room. It makes sense since Jessica skipped out without paying. Any chain hotel would do as much."

"You're right. Why should I do this?" She brought the cup up to hide her expression more than anything else. She didn't want him to know she'd been contemplating doing as much.

"I thought we could possibly trace the card from your end. Haven't had much experience doing this, but I thought it was worth a try. Maybe we could contact the credit card company and we'd at least know what the last charge was."

Donna responded. "You would if Jessica isn't running across the country charging everything. Still, that might help you track her. Yeah, I'd be glad to run the charge. I could pad out the bill for felonious activities while at my inn."

"Maybe you could put that underneath *No smoking in the rooms.* Is the satay done?"

The man was so obvious. He knew she'd forgotten to get it out of the fridge. "It will be."

Donna speared the chunks of chicken on bamboo skewers and poured the sauce in a deep bowl for microwaving.

Mark watched her as carefully as her dog. Both males depended on her for tasty food, although Jasper tended to be more apparent in his entreaties.

"Where's Daniel?" The detective picked up his cup for another sip.

"Your guess is as good as mine. I only know he was here earlier. I heard him laughing with the Babbles."

The front door slammed, making the attached bell jingle. Donna winced, knowing the exact price of the etched glass panels.

"Maybe that's him now." Mark twisted on the stool to face the interior door.

Her brother wouldn't have slammed the front door or used it for that matter.

The empty foyer emphasized the enraged woman's voice. "Where is she?"

It didn't take Donna more than one guess to figure out who it was. No, she knew. The swinging door flew inward as a red-faced Terri filled the doorway. Her glittering eyes slipped past Mark to fix on Donna. "I could kill you for that stunt."

Chapter Thirteen

C AUGHT. DONNA STARED at the woman who, given the slightest provocation, could lunge in her direction and possibly wrap her hands around her neck. It would be an excellent example of how far Terri would go. Still, Mark would know she'd provoke her and discount it as an emotional display.

Her former locker partner always underestimated her. She managed to blink twice before making a round O with her lips. "It wasn't there? I know your friends would have a party in your honor. It's possible whoever put the brochure together inserted the wrong restaurant." She managed to hold her incredulous expression while Mark wrinkled his nose.

The woman's flush dissipated as she held a finger up. "That's what happened. There aren't that many decent restaurants in town."

Donna didn't bother to point out that several new places had popped up in the intervening years.

"There's The Hitching Post," Terri said with a nod.

That place had gone out of business. The decent thing would be to tell her. Before her good angel and bad angel could battle it out, Mark interrupted.

"I have a few questions for you."

Terri cocked her head and managed a dismissive sniff. "Yes, I'm single. No, I'm not interested."

The slightly rumpled man brought a finger to his nose, hiding his expression. He coughed once, and then spoke. "No, my questions involve Wyn Lansing." He flashed his badge, which made Terri back up a few steps.

"Did that wannabe a country star wife of Wyn's sic you on me?" Before Mark could answer, the woman continued. "Talk to the woman Wyn checked in with. I kept my distance from the man knowing he was married."

Donna busied herself putting away dishes, knowing she wouldn't be able to keep a straight face.

"Ah, yes, but Wyn *did* enter your room and *passed* some time with you." Mark inserted the info without pointing out how he obtained it.

Even though her back was turned, Donna could still feel *the look* burning into her skin.

Terri retorted, "A little on the side isn't against the law."

"True," Mark agreed with a reasonable tone that fooled people into thinking he was on their side. "Where were you last night after 10 pm?"

Donna half-turned to put the plates in the cupboard. Terri stood perfectly still. Her eyes flickered upward. Nothing else moved, but Botox did make it hard to judge emotions.

"I was watching television," she murmured the words and then added, "Alone."

Mark nodded and asked, "Do you know anyone who'd want to hurt Wyn?"

He didn't mention anything about Wyn being dead. Terri's rapid departure had bypassed her hearing any news about the most recent development.

Again, the blank face. She sniffed before speaking. "The handsome charmer collects enemies who get between him and what he wants."

"What would he want?" Mark asked.

"Everything. The good life, money, fame, adoration. He doesn't care who he uses, either. He probably married his latest wife for money or to hatch another con."

Donna stopped moving, afraid she might distract Terri from dissing her boyfriend.

Mark continued to probe. "Did you know of any business that might have backfired?"

"Not exactly. He did mention he had something in the works that would have him relocating to a warmer climate. The man doesn't even trust me."

She spat the last word as if it were unbelievable. Wyn may have been a con man, but had enough sense not to trust Terri. The woman would insist on a cut of the profits.

"Anything else?"

Terri held her hands up and asked in a high-pitched voice. "Has something happened to Wyn?"

Why the woman had gotten the lead in the school plays befuddled her. She couldn't act if her life depended on it, which it might.

Mark slid his notebook out and jotted a few things in it. He answered while still looking at the notebook. "You could say that. He's dead."

Terri gasped, covered her mouth, and exited in a hurry. The swinging door swung back and forth in her wake.

Mark shook his head and asked, "Do you think she's really upset about Wyn?"

Donna pursed her lips, since she'd been wondering the same thing herself. "She'd give up the man in a heartbeat if it would benefit her. Still, they had shared memories. So, I'd say yes, except it's also her nature to be dramatic."

No reason to add cunning backstabber, since Mark already knew her feelings. How people remembered things were not how they actually happened. *Maybe Terri hadn't been that evil. The Pope wasn't Catholic, either.* Had Wyn bopped through life without a clue of how many people he'd stomped on to get what he wanted? Had someone not taken it lying down?

"Not the murderer," Mark concluded as he replaced his pen and notepad.

Seriously? "How can you say that? The woman's capable of murder." *Did he miss the part where Terri threatened to kill me?* She fisted her hands on her hips and shot him a look.

He held up his hand as if a shield that would repel the look. "I didn't say she wasn't capable. Anyone is capable under the right circumstances. There's no motive, though."

"How's that?" *The woman had looked guilty to her. Just like that, he decides her high school nemesis was blameless.* "Did you decide that because of her innocent face or surgical enhancements?"

Another man had fallen prey to Terri. The knowledge created an unexpected hurt that sparked her combative attitude.

Mark grimaced. "Really, Donna."

Embarrassed that she'd even mention it, she shrugged and allowed him to explain.

"Wells stuck a junior officer on combing the Internet for information on your guests. Terri was one of the easiest. Been married twenty plus years to a major corporate player, which explains the expensive surgeries. The fact she'd booked herself under her single name meant she wanted to play, but she definitely doesn't want to give up her easy life. The woman wore a showy cocktail ring on her ring finger to hide the ring line."

Darn it, she wanted her to be guilty. It would be Karmic justice. "Who then?"

Mark stepped closer. "Several possibilities, his wife, his mistress, his counterfeit contact, even Arnie."

"Not Arnie. I might suspect him if Terri was the one dead. He had nothing against the man."

The detective raised his eyebrows. "You're fairly protective of him. I thought the man was a pain."

Donna sucked in her lips. *He had her there.* "He's not that bad, rather like an annoying little brother. Why would you suspect him? He has a successful business. The man's a millionaire."

"Is he? Who told you he was a millionaire?"

Donna replayed conversations about the dog butler business. The only person who mentioned he was a millionaire was the man himself. "He's actually a nice person. He baked my cookies while I handled Lucinda." As far as a defense of his lack of culpability, it made no sense. The man hadn't even talked to Wyn. He had made a point of avoiding the man. That, however, would be a good thing if they were confederates. "You might as well suspect the Babbles."

"I don't. Their marital discord rings true. Of course, it could be someone outside the inn, too."

Donna crossed her fingers and hoped this was the case. The Painted Lady did not need a reputation as a place where murderers stay. Even a hookup hotel label was preferable.

"I hope it is."

"Me too, if only for your continual booking success. So, how about that satay?"

The mention of the forgotten dish had her checking the microwave. "It's lukewarm now."

"Bring it on."

Instead of insisting it should be served hot, she brought the plate and sauce over. "I want no complaints that it'd be better hot."

"You'll get none." The man hooked a stool with his foot, sat, picked up the bamboo-skewered chicken, and worked the meat off the stick. "This is my first real food in…" he hesitated, "…since your reception last night."

"You should eat more regular meals." She offered the advice, thinking she sounded more like a wife or a grandmother.

"I would if you could keep the crime wave down that you spawned with the opening of your business."

He delivered the remark in such a flat manner it was hard to tell if he was joking or not.

"I did not advertise for criminals. They just show up."

"Yeah, I know. It doesn't help that Herman keeps floating that tale about the diamonds. A dim bulb just might believe him."

"No one would be fooled by that urban legend."

The man raised one eyebrow as he chewed, possibly realizing her denial was a tad too strong. *Okay, maybe she believed the story a little.*

"Did you see any other odd behavior with your guests?" he asked.

The query made her laugh. "The most normal ones have to be the Babbles. She's upset because her sister-in-law is having a blowout wedding. As for her husband, he just wants another drink. Then there's the man who wants us to think he's Santa Claus."

"Don't discount that. Sometimes the best way to hide is not to."

"You have a point, but he seems relatively nice."

Mark quit chewing long enough to shoot her an *are you kidding me* stare.

"Where's Lucinda?" she asked to change the subject.

Mark picked up another loaded bamboo skewer. "Wells had her check into a motel up the road."

"The competition." It wasn't like the woman could take Wyn's empty room. "What about her?"

"Good question. She acted shocked, but that could only means she's a better actress than Terri."

Ah-ha! At least someone else agreed with her when it came to the ex-cheerleader's dramatic abilities. "She mentioned that Wyn's life insurance was still in the ex-wife's name." Donna held up a finger, knowing the man's objection. "She mentioned this while she was drinking, which means it's more likely to be true."

A disappointed sigh filled the room. "Here I thought you kept up with all the crime dramas. You have no clue how much it would take to make Lucinda tipsy. At best, she could be dropping information to muddy the trail. At worst, it's one more name to add to the list."

Not what she wanted to hear. "In all the crime dramas, it's always the least likely person."

Mark licked sauce off his thumb. "You do realize the least likely person would be you."

Chapter Fourteen

MARIA ZIPPED UP Donna's dress while commenting, "You look great. Arnie's eyes will bug out."

Donna certainly hoped not. The need to gather information on Wyn's associates served as her sole motivation. Mark pointed out that since it was her reunion it wouldn't attract attention if she attended. What was worse, she had to ask Arnie if he'd go as her date.

Due to their history, the good detective thought the two of them showing up together should stir up enough gossip to relax the culprit. That depended on the culprit attending. Jessica had probably made it across the Mexican border by now. In Donna's mind, the woman was the most likely suspect since she'd been Wyn's partner. She also was the only one who ran. It was an open and shut case.

Wells had shadowed Santa Ferguson and uncovered the man's preferences for dark ale and barmaids with elfin features. Another officer shadowed Dean and Marvin, who visited every antique shop within an eighty-mile radius. "Have the Babbles left for the wedding yet?"

Maria chuckled. "You missed it since you were getting ready. George had on one of those powder blue tuxes while his wife sported a sour look. I made sure to hide Jasper so they wouldn't take him."

"Thanks." At least she didn't need to worry about her dog. "Do you think I'm making a mistake going to the reunion with Arnie?

We're going on a dinner cruise. What if he's the killer? I'll be trapped on a boat. How do I even know if he's the Dog Butler Millionaire?"

"Having second thoughts? You defended the man fiercely according to Mark." Her sister-in-law held up some dangling earrings next to her face. At the time she had truly believed Arnie innocent. Not so much now. "I know. It hasn't even been a day, but I was hoping for a quick resolution. Crimes of passion are no-brainers. All the guests have alibis. Of course, most of their alibis were they were asleep at the time. No one knows I bunked in the pantry, but I slept like a rock."

"Donna!" Maria stopped picking through earrings to stare at her. "Why didn't you say anything?"

"I didn't hear anything. I locked the front door after Mark left and cleaned up the kitchen. I half-planned to go home, but I could barely stay awake. I also treated myself to a glass or two of the leftover wine."

Maria waved a finger at her. "Quit making excuses. I bet your original plan was to keep the lovebirds apart."

"Maybe. I fell into such a deep sleep I didn't wake up until my cell phone alarm went off. Normally, I wake up several times a night."

"Odd." Maria picked up the earrings again. "I slept hard, too. Daniel even commented on it."

Their eyes met. Donna offered the possibility first. "Drugged?"

"It's possible. It had to happen at the reception. Someone didn't want Wyn followed. Jessica?"

Maria looked unconvinced. "A person would show up at the reception to prove later that he or she had been drugged, too. Of course, they'd know what to avoid."

"What was something everyone ate or drank?" Donna wondered aloud. "I made up the desserts ahead of time and had the fridge locked."

"It could have been in the beverages."

The memory of Wyn and Terri in a corner toasting each other with wine glasses came to mind. "Wyn had a wine glass in his hand, I remember."

"It could have been something else. When would someone have had a chance to contaminate anything?"

Eunice had volunteered to carry out platters. She'd plenty of time with the food. "Oh my goodness, it was Eunice. I have to tell Mark. No reason for me to go on the reunion cruise."

Donna reached for her phone to call Mark, but her sister-in-law grabbed the cell from her. "Stop. Eunice has no connections to Wyn."

"True." She held her hand out for her phone. Her sister-in-law gave her a suspicious glance before placing it back in her hand. Her thumb rested over Mark's speed dial number. "Geesh, Maria don't you watch the BBC mysteries? The little old ladies are always murderers."

She danced back as her determined relative made another grab for the phone, telling her, "You promised Arnie you'd go with him. Go ahead, make the man happy. I'll explain your Eunice theory to Mark. I doubt the woman could have made it across the rough terrain where he was found, though"

Not what she wanted to hear. She couldn't even say when she last went out on a date. She could use the practice. "I'll go only if you contact Mark from my house as opposed to the inn. We've already experienced what a sneak Eunice can be. Even now she could be getting rid of the evidence."

"I will. Still, the worst the woman could be guilty of is an overactive imagination. It has to be Jessica or the former wife." Maria reluctantly agreed and handed her the gold earrings. "Is Arnie meeting you here or at the inn?"

Her heart skipped a beat back when she considered that she had given the man, a possible murderer, her home address. "Here. Text me in two hours to make sure I'm still alive. If you get some polite text back, then you know the man pushed me overboard."

"You're really worried, aren't you?" Maria sounded surprised that her belligerent sister-in-law could be afraid.

The doorbell rang, ending whatever she might say. Her front-facing bedroom allowed her to peek through the blinds to see a long black limousine in her driveway. "Maybe the man really is a millionaire."

After fastening on her earrings, she strolled to the door with her turquoise tea length chiffon dress floating behind her. She opened the door to a formally dressed Arnie, holding a sheaf of roses.

"Oh, these are beautiful. I'll have to put them in water." Maria appeared by her side and took the flowers. "You two go have fun."

Arnie offered her his arm, and they proceeded to the limo where a uniformed driver stood at attention by the open door.

Donna knew her neighbors were peeking through the curtains. It would be nice to have something pleasant whispered about her. "You shouldn't have."

He patted her hand resting on the crook of his arm. "Indulge me. I always wanted to treat you like a queen, even if it's only for one night."

The man hadn't mistaken her invitation to accompany her to the reunion as a case of infatuation. "I have to say no one has ever done that."

"They should have." He nodded at the driver as they both slid into the back.

Soft music played inside. A magnum of champagne chilled in an ice bucket. Tiny lights outlined the tinted windows, resembling miniature stars against the black upholstery. The residual scent of the roses perfumed the air. The atmosphere eased her nervous stomach that had begun acting up as soon as Mark suggested the reunion plan. The driver closed the window between them and started the car.

Arnie intertwined his fingers with hers and smiled. He really wasn't a bad looking man, especially when seated. Why hadn't she liked him in high school?

"So, Donna, is the policewoman posing as your cousin supposed to keep everyone in the inn or just watch them?"

Yeah, now she remembered. The man was clueless about what to say when. How could she have forgotten? The same way she had blocked out Pat, the policewoman, being at the inn along with Daniel, although she doubted Pat would need Daniel's help. She'd put her money on the policewoman if it ever came to a fight.

"Ah, Pat, she came up from Charleston to help for the weekend."

Arnie gave her the same disbelieving look she directed at newbie nurses when they asked how to do basic procedures. "What?"

"She has a Brooklyn accent."

"People move, you know."

He smirked and brought her hand up to his lips for a kiss. "You're adorable when you lie."

No one had ever told her that before. Maybe the man wasn't as socially ill adept as she thought.

"Champagne?"

His breath feathered her hand as he asked.

"Yes, please." It would keep his hands busy, too. She hadn't considered she'd be fending off Arnie. Part of her wondered why she bothered.

They gently clinked their flutes. "Here's to a delightful evening," Donna proposed, thinking she sounded non-committal, not mentioning anything about checking out the other attendees. Besides, if Arnie were guilty, Mark would never have suggested she'd attend the reunion with him.

Arnie's eyes flickered with amusement as he offered his own toast. "Here's to this river cruise not being another Carrie re-enactment."

There he went again with the wrong words. "What?" She sipped the bubbly, mentally placing it in the good to excellent category. The man chose well.

"Ah, yes, you didn't attend that last dance on the paddle wheeler. I think that's why they chose a boat for tonight."

The limousine slowed and the dividing window came down an inch for the driver to announce, "We're here."

"Good," Arnie answered and took a final sip of the champagne before placing it in the cup holder. "Be back in two hours. The boat should be docked by then."

There was a flurry of door opening and wide-eyed fellow attendees nudging one another while she and Arnie proceeded up the gangway. Several people broke away from the group to talk to Arnie. Most of them pretended not to know her despite her seeing them in backless hospital gowns. It took a while before she could get the man alone to finish their discussion. Money or the appearance of money certainly attracted hangers-on. "Let's go up on deck for a stroll."

"A moonlight stroll." He purred the words and winked.

It was hard to know if his actions were for everyone else or herself. Technically, she should be making friendly and grilling people. Mark didn't want anyone to know that Wyn was dead. Of course, that would mean shipping Terri out of the county. A quick glance showed no signs of the attention-getting ex-cheerleader.

They slipped up the stairs, attracting some eyes as they went. A strong breeze greeted them as they opened the exterior door. A crescent moon hung in the sky, casting meager light onto the water. It would have been romantic if not for the stinky fish smell.

All she wanted was facts, not sweet nothings whispered into her ear. "Tell me about the dance? The one on the paddle wheeler."

"Here I thought you got me out here for a kiss." He chuckled at his own perceived wit, patting her hand. "I was surprised you weren't at the dance."

Donna tried to remember what had been her excuse at the time. Her goal had been to grab one of the elusive full ride scholarships that didn't happen by popping off to every dance her school had. Someone had asked her. It might have been Arnie. "Did you ask me?"

He gave her a curt nod. "You palmed me off with the writing scholarship essays excuse."

"I did write the essays."

He grabbed her hand when the boat gave a small rock. "I figured that out when I didn't see you at the dance. Apparently, Wyn and Terri thought it would be great fun to get some gullible girl to attend with Wyn. They'd even lined up red paint to dump on the girl. Turns out someone warned the girl. It wasn't like the two of them were good at keeping secrets. I'm surprised the school administrators knew nothing about it. If they did, they did nothing to stop it."

Arnie continued. "The boat was crowded that night due to so many students wanting to see the spectacle. Terri was not a happy camper when Wyn showed up alone. I secretly breathed a sigh of relief for the girl."

"You warned her, didn't you?"

"Guilty." He managed to look embarrassed in the dim light.

"That's sweet. I underestimated you. Do you remember her name?"

How upset would a person be at a stunt pulled years ago? It would have been worse if it had been completed.

"Let me think. I might be able to remember it. It has been years ago. I may not have been a football star or even a scholar, but I've always had a good memory."

The soft snick of a gun cocking had Donna spinning to face Lorena Fitzgerald pointing a small pistol at Arnie. She told him, "I do feel bad about shooting you since you did me a favor back then, but I suspected you wouldn't be able to stop yourself from bragging to your crush. However, the name was actually Laura Gerald. I didn't want to change it entirely because I wanted Wyn to know who killed him and why. You remember everything that happened that night, and I can't allow the story to be brought up." She moved the pistol to target Donna. "I have no bone to pick with you. I would even go so far as to say you run a nice inn."

She had to take a compliment where she could get one. "Thank you. Feel free to vanish into the night. My memory isn't that good."

The woman gave a harsh laugh. "Yeah, right," she snarled, but kept her attention on Donna.

The split second of inattention was what Arnie needed. Head down, he plowed into Lorena who tumbled to the deck, but she somehow kept possession of her gun. A boom, high-pitched whine, and acrid scent had Donna ducking and weaving, unsure if her next breath might be her last. Her knees slammed onto the deck as she huddled against it, making herself a smaller target. Under the barrier of her arm, Donna watched as Lorena shifted into a crouching position for better aiming. Arnie dashed across the deck, trying to deflect attention away from Donna. A quick glance revealed nothing at hand to throw at the woman except her own stiletto heels. Sweat beaded her lip as her fingers tighten on her pump. A hard throw landed the shoe upside Lorena's head, which caused her to drop the gun and curse.

"What are you doing?" Lorena glared at Donna, who held up the other shoe threateningly. "I'd think you'd be on my side."

Arnie moved silently behind Lorena, heading for the gun a few feet out of reach. She had to distract her murderous guest. "Why would I be on your side?"

Lorena blinked as if confused by her words. "Everyone knows you were left at the altar."

Seriously? "Does everyone know?" Donna's hands shot up in aggravation, almost forgetting her need to keep Lorena's attention on her. "Why should that make me on your side?"

"Surely, you must know. I was in love with Wyn, even though the man was secretive about it. We were lovers. I thought he felt the same way."

Donna kept her eyes on the wild-eyed woman while tracking Arnie's crawl toward the gun. The weapon was about a foot out of his reach and almost the equal distance from Lorena. Either one could reach the gun. Depending on who obtained it would determine if Donna lived long enough to install an elevator in the inn.

"So you knew nothing about Wyn and Terri?"

The woman shook her head, sucking in a noisy breath. "I was so naïve. Wyn told me the two of them had broken up. I believed him. It seemed right that he'd ask me to the dance. He promised to announce our romance. Then, when Arnie showed up at my house to explain the real story, I knew I'd been a fool."

Arnie clutched the weapon the same time Lorena spun around looking for him.

He brandished the pistol, pointing it at the deceived lover. "I did you a favor, and you tried to kill me for it. I thought you a better person than that. Come to think of it, I don't even remember seeing you after the dance."

The woman's shoulders slumped as she heaved a deep sigh. Donna almost felt sorry for her, but it could all be an act.

Lorena's head jerked back up. A gleam appeared in her eyes as she walked toward Arnie. "Go ahead and shoot me. I've nothing to live for. You probably guessed, I never returned to school. I couldn't at first due to the humiliation. Once I found out I was pregnant my parents signed the paperwork for me to drop out of school."

The woman kept moving toward Arnie, daring him to shoot her. Donna knew he wouldn't. Stalling, she asked, "What happen to your child?"

Lorena stopped at the question and glanced back at Donna as if she'd forgotten she was even there. A wistful look transformed her features. "Ah, little Teddy. He was a handsome boy, not too surprising when you consider his father. He was my entire life. I'd ended up working the night shift at a hotel, barely making ends meet, living with my mother, when Teddy was diagnosed with cancer."

Arnie took the opportunity to back up a few steps, which was good. Lorena would rip the gun out of his hands as soon as she got close enough.

"Did..." Donna hesitated, wondering if the wrong question would direct her attention back to Arnie whom she was beginning to believe really wouldn't hurt a fly. "…Teddy survive?"

"No, he didn't. I even contacted Wyn for help with the medical bills and the possibility he might want to see his son. He told me he had no clue who I was because he didn't remember all the women he'd slept with. When I mentioned Teddy, he laughed and told me I couldn't pin it on him."

Donna could picture the man saying exactly that. "That must have hurt. I can understand why you were angry."

"Devastated. That naïve part of me thought Wyn would step up to help. He'd meet Teddy, who would get better, and things would have a happy ending."

Did Terri know all this? Did Wyn even mention it? Donna's lips twisted as she considered what questions would keep the woman talking. "When did you plan your revenge?"

Lorena breathed deeply as if considering her reply. "It's been a good thirty years. I'd have upswings when I didn't consider any revenge at all. I went back to school, even got my MBA. Married briefly, but my husband died."

Did her husband die or was he helped? The woman kept talking, staring at Donna, but not seeing her. "No kids and no husband gave me more than enough leisure time to follow Wyn's life. No matter what he did, the man always came out on top. No justice. I decided to make my own."

Where was everyone? Shouldn't someone have heard the gun shot? Mark promised her that there would be a security detail to keep her safe. "How did you plan it?"

Arnie gave her a thumb up when she glanced his way, whatever that was supposed to mean.

A slow smile broke across Lorena's face. "It was easy. I called him up, told him I had a crush on him. Refused to tell him my name or give him my number. I made sure my number was private so he couldn't call me back. I held the power." She gestured to herself.

An unknown admirer would intrigue any man if he hadn't watched any of those fatal attraction news programs. "Did you tell him you'd meet him at the reunion?"

"I did." Lorena nodded and folded her arms, appearing calm, even resigned.

Looks can be deceiving. Both she and Arnie needed to be prepared for when she flipped out since it didn't look like the cavalry was coming. "How'd you work that with Wyn showing up with Jessica and Terri on the side?"

The woman shifted her weight as she chafed her arms. "I didn't expect that. I should have, though, after how he treated me. I stayed in my room. I called him from my cell and lured him out of the inn. I stayed about a quarter mile in front of him, always telling him a block or two farther. He started to balk when he came to the woods."

Lorena smirked. "I promised something special if he'd come a bit farther. We met by the creek in almost no light."

"You killed him when he couldn't see you?" It would explain him falling forward in the stream without a struggle.

A small snort sounded. "Of course not, I shot him when he told me he didn't know a Laura Gerald. The man ruined my life, and he didn't even remember my name. He deserved to be shot."

Wyn may have deserved something, but killing wasn't it.

A tear slid down Lorena's face. She slowly slid to her knees and started crying. *Were they real tears?* A commotion near the end of the deck drew her focus. Several uniformed police officers and Mark Taber streamed out of the doorway.

"Donna, are you okay?" Mark shouted, as the two police officers sprinted forward and cuffed Lorena.

The woman sobbed louder. "I killed the only man I ever loved."

Mark pulled on latex gloves and took the gun from Arnie, who slumped against the railing after handing it over. "Appreciate your help, Forrester."

"No problem." He gave a small salute.

Mark held out his arm to her. "You ready to go?"

Did he really have to ask? She tucked her hand in the bend of his arm and padded beside him in her stocking feet. "Do you wonder now why I hate reunions?

Chapter Fifteen

DANIEL LEANED AGAINST the counter as Donna bustled around the kitchen, pulling together a quiet dinner as a thank you for keeping the murder far away from the inn. She checked the leg of lamb, which was browning up nicely, and Mark should be here any minute.

Her brother continued to summarize each guest's exit. "The Babbles left, arguing as they went, clueless that a murder happened during their stay. I kept hold of your dog until they left the premises."

Her eyes went to the corner of the room where Jasper was snoozing. "What happened to Terri?"

The question made him laugh. "Good thing you were gone or you'd have felt her rage. She got all dolled up for the reunion, but literally missed the boat due to a sobriety checkpoint. Came back ranting, then came down the stairs ten minutes later and checked out."

"Pat didn't stop her?"

Her brother's lips twisted as he shook his head. "Not sure how she could."

"The rest of the guests?" She checked on her risotto, which could use a dash of nutmeg.

"Hmm, none of them were nearly as colorful." Daniel put one hand out as he counted off the guests. "Dean and Marvin told me they'd be back."

"Good. I like them. Could you open the red wine for me?"

Her brother uncorked the wine as he talked. "Strange thing happened with our Christmas obsessed gentleman."

"What?" Her imagination ran rampant, imagining the seasonal chaos the man could have caused. "Did he paint tiny elves above the door sills?"

Her brother cocked his head as if her suggestion was on the peculiar side. "No, he befriended Lucinda. When he packed up his wares, Lucinda arrived to help him. The two of them left, talking as if they'd be friends forever."

The lone counterfeit bill had her considering money laundering scenarios involving Lucinda and the Christmas salesman. Sure, Wyn was dead, his killer caught, but the counterfeiters were still out there. Thank goodness, no one paid her in cash.

A business card appeared in front of her face, courtesy of her brother. "Arnie asked me to give you his card. He told me to tell you to call him anytime. Looks like you stole another heart."

"Yeah, I'm a regular femme fatale." The thought generated a smile as she slid the salads out of the fridge. "What happened to Eunice?"

"Yeah, that. I'll let Herman explain that one." Daniel headed for the back door and held up his hand in a wave.

By the time, she had the table set, a rap sounded at her backdoor. She had unlocked it, expecting company. "Come in," she called out in a congenial voice. Not too romantic, but just enough warmth to make a man want to open the door.

The sound of footsteps made her smile to herself. It had been a long time since she had planned a romantic dinner. An even longer time since she actually carried the plans through. Now that the man was here, she wasn't too sure of herself.

"I'm glad you came." She turned and was surprised to see Herman, her neighbor.

"Pleased to hear it, especially knowing what I have to say."

Please, not another episode of the Lowery Diamonds mystery. She didn't have the time. "I'm kinda in a hurry here."

Herman sniffed the air. "I can tell, but I need to tell you, especially if you plan on drinking any wine tonight."

Her neighbor wouldn't be going anywhere unless she heard him out. "Go on." She gestured for him to continue.

"Remember the wine and cheese to-do?"

It was less than a week ago. "I remember everyone slept well afterward." Make that almost everyone. "Why do I have a feeling I'm not going to like this?"

Herman winced a little. "Eunice drugged the wine and ice water so she could look for the diamonds while everyone was asleep. She had some prescription sleeping pills she dissolved into the liquid. Liquor and medicine can make a potent combination."

"That would explain a great deal. Eunice didn't tell me herself, because...?" She had her suspicions.

"Something about you pressing charges and taking away her discount. Besides, she fell asleep and didn't do anything. Her daughter showed up and took her back to the home." He shuffled his feet and cleared his throat. "Please don't be too hard on her. The bad girls can't help what they are. They're irresistible, too." The man's bemused expression changed as Mark wandered into the room without knocking. "Who's irresistible?"

Herman's eyebrows shot up. "Never mind." He made a dash for the door, then stopped and looked back. "Don't drink any wine unless you need a good night's sleep."

"Surely, not all the wine."

Herman's response was the door slamming. Donna walked to the door and locked it. Maybe having wine laced with sleeping pills wouldn't be such a bad thing. Guests might write about what a wonderful night's sleep they had. It certainly would save on throwing out the wine.

She gestured to the door. "Herman informed me Eunice put sleeping pills into the wine and ice water. Makes me wonder how Wyn even made it to the woods."

"Wells discovered the man was a long-term member of Alcoholic Anonymous. He may have come in late and pretended to drink"

"Makes sense. Still…" She thought of Eunice prowling through her house while she had slept. "What about Eunice?"

"Ha! I remember she wanted a particular wine, but she must have forgotten or didn't know the difference." He waggled his eyebrows at the elderly woman's persnickety ways. "I poured her two glasses."

"Maybe she left one bottle untainted, and that's the one she wanted." She didn't know how much of a wine connoisseur the woman was. The names often sounded alike, which could be confusing. "Which one did she want?"

Mark shrugged. "The Chardonnay I'd already emptied. I wrapped a towel around another bottle and pretended that was it. No complaints, which meant she couldn't tell the difference."

"You saved my floor boards from being pulled up with that stunt." The idea of a diamond hungry Eunice attacking her house with a crowbar made her shiver.

"Cold?" Mark whispered near her ear.

"Just thinking what could have happened. Let me get dinner on the table."

The thoughtful detective helped her ferry out the lamb and risotto. The salads and bread were already on the table along with flickering candles to give the room a romantic air. Donna debated if she should bring in the flourless chocolate torte when Mark entered with the bottle of wine and poured them both a glass.

"To us," he proposed in a toast.

Donna clinked her glass against his. "And staying awake the entire meal."

The End

Donna's Fast Pate & Cranberry Bites

Go to your local grocery and buy liver pate. Not sure where to find it, ask at the deli.

On to the cranberry apple jelly, which you do have to make. This can be made ahead and used on toast too.

Ingredients for Jelly
- 2 Tbsp. Dried cranberries
- ½ cup Cranberry sauce (the kind that holds the shape of the can)
- ½ cup Apple juice, (clear)
- 1 tsp Gelatin (the non-flavored kind)
- ½ cup Water

1. For the jelly, combine the cranberry sauce, dried cranberries and apple juice and bring to a gentle simmer.
2. Meanwhile, sprinkle gelatin over the water and let it swell for 2 minutes, then add into the hot cranberries mixture and stir until dissolved.
3. Meanwhile, allow the pate to reach room temperature. Press into a shallow bowl or pan.
4. Allow to cool for 10 minutes before spooning on top of the pâté.
5. Chill and allow to set for at least 1 hour.
6. Before company arrives, place the chilled bowl on a serving platter with toasted brioche fingers, sourdough or crackers. Don't forget to add the serving knives or spoon.

Impress the Detective Leg of Lamb

Ingredients

- 1 (7-pound) semi-boneless leg of lamb, aitchbone removed, fat trimmed to 1/4 inch thick, and lamb tied (Local is better)
- 4 garlic cloves
- 1 tablespoon fine sea salt
- 2 tablespoons chopped fresh rosemary
- ½ teaspoon black pepper
- ¼ cup dry red wine* or beef broth

Preparation

1. Pat lamb dry and score fat by making shallow cuts all over with tip of a sharp small knife. This will keep the meat moist while cooking.
2. Pound garlic to a paste with sea salt using a mortar and pestle. (Feel superior if you have a mortar and pestle. If not use that heavy chef knife from the wooden knife holder.) Stir together with rosemary and pepper. Put lamb in a lightly oiled roasting pan, and then rub paste all over lamb. Let stand at room temperature 30 minutes.
3. Preheat oven to 350°F.
4. Roast lamb in middle of oven until a meat thermometer inserted 2 inches into thickest part of meat (do not touch bone) registers 130°F, 1 1/2 to 1 3/4 hours. Transfer to a cutting board and let stand 15 to 25 minutes (internal temperature will rise to about 140°F for medium-rare).
5. Add wine to pan and deglaze by boiling over moderately high heat, stirring and scraping up brown bits, 1 minute. Season pan juices with salt and pepper and serve with lamb.

(This makes me hungry just typing it.)

*This is an excellent opportunity to use the wine you don't like.

Serves: 8

No Fuss Mini Manchego Tarts

(There are great for a fast appetizer. Although Donna is a purist and would never use the pre-shaped shells or at least she wouldn't tell anyone she did.)

Makes: 5-6 Servings

<u>Ingredients</u>

- 1 (1.9-ounce) package frozen mini phyllo pastry shells
- 1 cup finely grated manchego or Mahón cheese (about 2 ounces)
- 3 to 4 tablespoons tomato chutney or mango chutney
- Garnish: fresh marjoram leaves

1. Preheat oven to 400°. Arrange phyllo shells on a baking sheet. Divide grated cheese evenly among shells, and top each with a rounded ½ teaspoonful of chutney.
2. Bake at 400° for 5 to 8 minutes or until bubbly. Garnish with a few small marjoram leaves, if desired, and serve tartlets.

Ready for a Sneak Peek at Killer Review?

The Painted Lady Inn Mysteries

Killer Review

By M. K. Scott

J. E. MUSCOVY COULD destroy a restaurant and kill a chef's career with a sentence or two in one of her cutthroat reviews. The acerbic summations not only appeared in the top papers, but also were available online and for a phone app. Former popular eateries' clientele would thin out almost to the point of non-existence after a visit from J.E.

On the other hand, a career could experience a major boost if J.E. deemed a restaurant as good, even to the point of praising particular dishes. Those in the food world whispered a good review from J.E. always preceded a Michelin star, the gold standard in the culinary world. No wonder chefs longed for and feared a visit from the mercurial reviewer.

Donna stared at the laptop. She blinked, but it was still there. Daniel touched her shoulder as he went by, but instead of addressing her, he called out to his wife.

"Maria, I think a pod person has taken my sister's place. All she does is stare at the computer screen in total silence."

Her sister-in-law's tinkling laughter irritated Donna. Didn't anyone realize how serious this was?

"I think she's in shock. Her idol may have booked a room."

While she usually enjoyed Muscovy's no-holds barred reviews, she'd never been at the receiving end of one. Janice, a nurse turned chef, alerted her to the reviewer's visit. Somehow, the woman knew everything in the food world, even when the health inspector would arrive. Thankfully, she tipped off Donna before arrival and what their target focus would be.

Janice's colorful bistro, The Croaking Frog, might merit a visit from the illustrious reviewer. Even though it didn't boast the label fine dining, it had appeared on The Food Channel as a hidden gem. The locals who kept the place in the red during the lean years found it hard to get in with the influx of so many foodies checking out the place.

The town had become a hot spot for food tourists since not one, but two fine dining restaurants decided to locate here. Sylvester's Salon was a pretentious place with waiters who could out snob the queen. Despite the inflated price, an entrée didn't provide enough food to feed a toddler. Janice joked in the beginning that most of her customers came directly from Sylvester's to her place since they hadn't received enough to eat.

Sylvester's competition came in the form of Norelle's, an upscale Cajun restaurant. The words upscale and Cajun should have been an oxymoron when put together, but it wasn't. The interior was kitschy with dark touches such as the grinning crystal skulls at the bar to remind people even good times were temporary. Norelle's prices were as high as Sylvester's, but the portions were significantly larger, which created a strong customer base.

Another morbid draw was the wall of death. It didn't apply to anyone who managed to consume a thirty-two ounce porterhouse steak similar to the photos of red-faced patrons that steakhouses featured. Oh no, Norelle's was much worse. Near a dark corner, the wall took an odd swing as if someone tried to build a secret alcove, but wasn't too covert about it. On the short wall were black and white photos of celebrities and dignitaries, dead ones. The popular establishment did start in New Orleans so they could have visited the restaurant once, but she didn't think so. All she knew was a new photo went up a day or two *before* someone died. They always died, which was creepy. It also kept her from examining the wall too closely, just in case her photo showed up.

A cup of coffee appeared near the laptop along with her brother pulling up a stool to the kitchen island. "Give it a break. You don't know that the Jane Ellen Muscovy who booked online is your mysterious poison pen reviewer."

She shot her brother a look of disbelief. "Janice confirmed it. You know she has moles everywhere."

Maria balanced a stack of empty snack baskets on her hip as she strolled by and added her two cents. "If Janice Cunningham tells you something, believe it. That woman could run a crime family or a spy organization single-handedly. I'm not sure she doesn't. She probably tells the staff at Norelle's who will die next."

Daniel snorted. "Please? Have you all gone crazy? One solitary woman picked the inn to stay at and the two of you start weaving tales."

Men sometimes couldn't see what was right in front of them. "Solitary single woman, that's it. It would be different if she had a companion. Then it might be a vacation. If I had a bunch of single women, then it would be a girls weekend. Make a note, we should offer girls weekend. Maria, what should we offer for the girls weekend?"

"Mmm." Her sister-in-law hesitated, before answering as she arranged brownies, cookies, and individual-sized snack bags of chips and crackers in the baskets. "Wine, discounts at the local spa, maybe a free gift, perhaps you could get Janice to throw in a buy one get one meal free coupon?"

The back door swung open letting in the cool autumn air as Tennyson entered with Jasper. Donna held up her hand to her live-in helper. While the boy worked practically free any attempt at conversation resulted in a long existential discussion about the meaning of life. What did she expect from a philosophy major?

He wasn't her first choice for the job with his mournful expression as if his soul hurt along with his shoes. Truthfully, he was her only candidate. A tiny bedroom, a pocket size bathroom in the laundry room, free Wi-Fi, and two meals a day along with sixty dollars a week wasn't the lure Daniel thought it would be.

Tennyson had the nerve to complain about her cable package. She'd almost given the male the boot before he'd even started, but Jasper liked him. Dogs were supposed to be good judges of character, but it was hard to remember someone Jasper didn't like.

Her brother greeted Tennyson. "How's it hanging?"

Really. That would be the nail in her B and B coffin if J.E. were here. She'd devoted a paragraph about a restaurant where the coat check girl and hostess had debated the paternity of a child. The place instead of getting a star, got a V for vulgar.

A long sigh answered his query. Good. She didn't have time for a soliloquy on the deplorable state of humanity or some circular logic about a man only thinking he existed, but didn't in reality. The bluebird of unhappiness would arrive anytime.

"I better recheck all the rooms."

She'd moved Jane Ellen into her best room, hers. Why she even went to the trouble to make the room hers mystified her since she spent more time removing her stuff as opposed to actually using the ground floor room.

Her brother's voice stopped her before she hit the swinging door to the foyer.

"Your mysterious single woman could just be here to conduct an illicit affair with a married man."

Her eyes rolled upward. Daniel thought that was the bright side? She used her key to give her room one final check. The fresh flower arrangement she'd asked Maria to pick up looked good, except for the lilies and carnations. She plucked out the two small lilies and the three carnations. A careful relocation of the greenery hid any holes the plucked flowers might have caused.

The offensive flowers she'd hide in the outside dumpster so Maria wouldn't see them. She didn't want to explain how she always viewed carnations and lilies as funeral flowers along with the peace palm. The last thing she needed at the inn was anything that smacked of death or funerals.

Voices in the hall alerted her that a guest had already arrived. An unfamiliar woman's voice twined with Daniel's. Donna cradled the rejected flowers in the crook of one arm rather like a beauty contest winner. Maria stood behind the table typing in the needed information. Tennyson slid into the room sporting a shirt that read "Kill Yourself Now and Spare Yourself the Pain".

Donna's eyes almost popped out. *Where did that come from?* Under the guise of being helpful, she offered to do Tennyson's laundry and deep sixed most of his shirts. She replaced them with similar plain T-shirts, hoping he might think the depressing messages vanished in the high heat dryer. He'd never said anything, but then he went out and bought more. In the dictionary, there had to be a snapshot of Tennyson next to the passive-aggressive definition.

He might offer to carry the woman's luggage as she'd prompted him to do, even hinting he might get a tip for his trouble. The last thing she needed was Jane Ellen taking a look at his T-shirt and giving the inn an A as in places to avoid. The reviewer was big on using letter detonations.

Of course, the middle-aged woman dressed all in black might not be the critic. She could be here for a mortuary conference or a reunion for aging Goths. Everyone knew New Yorkers always wore black, at least that's what Janice said. It was easy to pick them out even in the sultry summer months since they still sported their dark garments. It was almost like a uniform so they could identify one another in an emergency.

Her rapid gait almost approached a jog, but not quite. Donna pasted a smile on her face while cutting her eyes to Tennyson, warning him not to move. His eyebrows drew together in confusion, confirming he'd received her message and stepped back into the kitchen.

"Welcome to the Painted Lady Inn," she enthused, causing everyone to look her way.

Her brother wiggled his eyebrows. The woman's unsmiling countenance suggested she was indeed the critic. A judgmental glance started at Donna's head and swept downward to her toes. Ah, she wondered if any food was on her face. Maybe her hair was sticking up from checking under the beds. After a lengthy silence, the woman smiled.

"You brought me flowers. How nice. Lilies and carnations, my favorites."

Donna had no choice, but to give her the offensive flowers as if that had been her original intention. No surprise, blooms normally seen at funeral homes would suit the critic. Perhaps she threw a carnation on the smoking wreckage of a dream she destroyed. "I could put them in an arrangement in your room, if you'd like."

"Ah, yes, I would like that. A small glass of your best sherry would suit, too."

Maria held up the room key, her eyes flicking between Donna and Daniel. Her brother grasped the key and swept up the suitcase, leading the parade to the room. Jane Ellen followed her brother.

"How long has your inn been in operation?"

Daniel threw a grin over his shoulder. The same expression before his marriage melted more than one feminine heart. "Oh, almost a year, now."

"Really?" The woman angled her head, taking in the stairs and an ornate painting in the hall that depicted a Victorian woman and her two children in a garden setting. She gestured to the image. "Is the family portrait part of the inn's history?"

Her brother, who never had a clue where the various items came from, didn't answer immediately. Perhaps he was debating about revealing the inn's checkered past, including its stint as a VFW and a destination for murder.

Donna moved a step closer. "It could be the original builder's wife. The general story is that he built the house as a labor of love for his new wife." Actually, Herman had revealed the place was a showy piece of architecture built to show the owner's prestige.

Remembering a scathing review citing how one of her second-floor bedrooms was so pink it irritated the guest had future visitors requesting not to have the pink room. New floral curtain and changing out a chair made it less pink. Yeah, she could see why Janice feared the woman's visit.

The woman might decide to write a review on The Painted Lady Inn. With that in mind, she'd have to do backflips to keep the woman happy. She poked the flowers back into the arrangement while Daniel explained the breakfast times. "We'd be happy to bring breakfast to your room."

The woman waved them both away. "No breakfast. My job is to judge food. I can't have pedestrian cuisine confusing my palate, which is the tool I use in my profession. My body is a temple. Now, where's my sherry?"

Yeah, temple. Donna hotfooted it out of the room before she said something aloud. The only sherry in the house was cooking sherry. She'd have to stop Maria before she poured it into an aperitif glass.

No sign of her sister-in-law in the kitchen, although Tennyson stared at a half-filled glass of water. He called it contemplation. She snorted when he explained he was receiving sympathetic vibrations from the liquid.

"Tennyson, where's Maria?"

The college junior startled. His hand slipped on its perch on the island, causing him to contemplate the water much closer before he stopped his descent with his other hand. Ha, exactly as she thought. The male had mastered the elusive art of sleeping with his eyes open.

He blinked twice confirming her initial thought. "Whadya say?"

"Maria. Where is she?"

The young man's brow furrowed as if trying to analyze her words for some hidden meaning. She was about to restate the question when the back door opened. A breathless Maria rushed into the kitchen, clutching an ornate glass bottle in one hand.

"I found some. Herman keeps some quality sherry to impress the ladies. I remember him saying that once."

Donna blew out a breath. Someone paid attention to Herman's various stories. Though not a sherry fan, she could remember it was served in small glasses since it was more potent than regular wine.

"Thank goodness. I don't know anything about sherry except little old ladies drank it in the old black and white movies. Get online and see if we are supposed to serve something with it like wafers."

Her sister-in-law chuckled as she reached for the laptop stored in the cabinet. "It's not communion. I never heard of it served with anything." The sound of light finger tapping replaced her words.

Donna rolled the bottle in her hand, looked for a bottling stamp that would clue her to the age of the beverage. No doubt. The critic waiting impatiently for her drink would know in one sip.

"Uh oh." Maria glanced up from the computer. "We have a problem."

Having a cut-throat critic in her inn wasn't enough of a problem. Donna inhaled, closed her eyes, and mentally counted to ten. The action was supposed to calm her. She opened her eyes and nodded for what had to be unwelcome information.

Maria turned the laptop screen in her direction. There was a long list of varying temperatures for sherry to be served depending on its specific type. In the end, the liquor had to be chilled, and the bottle in her hand was room temperature. "We're screwed."

"It's in metric, too. Who can figure out this stuff out?"

Tennyson leaned to look at the screen. "I can read it. What type of sherry do you have?"

Her woebegone helper could speak in something other than rhetorical question. He could also interpret metric, which was never a skill she even considered useful until now. She held the bottle up to the light to better read the label. "It's a dry Amontillado."

"That's thirteen in Celsius." Maria relayed the information.

A slight pause punctuated the conversation. "That would be about fifty-six degrees." Tennyson grinned as he delivered the information. "That means it is only slightly lower than room temperature. All you need to do is wrap a wet paper towel around it and put it in the freezer for a few minutes."

Her surprise at this stranger who had taken over her helper's body kept her silent, but not Maria.

"Isn't the Amontillado wine the one in the Edgar Allan Poe story?"

It probably wasn't something she needed to think about. If a damp paper towel cooled down a bottle fast, she'd use a dishtowel. That had to be faster.

The two of them chattered on about a man being bricked up in a wall as she placed the wine in the freezer. How long should she leave it? Wouldn't J.E. be looking for it? The fact her brother hadn't returned meant he was busy turning on the charm. Daniel taught her one thing. Women responded favorably when a handsome man chatted them up.

The door swung open, revealing her red-faced brother. "Where's the sherry? That woman was quizzing me on the inn and made derogatory sounds when I didn't answer the questions to her satisfaction. I felt like I was back in Sister Mary Ellen's class. I'm surprised she didn't whip a ruler out of her suitcase to slap my hands for unsatisfactory conduct."

Donna met Maria's surprised gaze. Daniel's charm was legendary—until now.

"Pour her a huge snifter," Daniel encouraged. "You might want to throw her some raw meat, too."

A quick pivot allowed her to hide a smile. Her brother met a woman who hadn't hung on his every word. Sure, it was petty of her, but sometimes she just wanted her brother to live in the same world she did. A quick detour to the large utility drawer would net the food thermometer. At least, it measured in Fahrenheit and Celsius. The space where she kept it in the metal organizer was empty.

"My thermometer is missing." Great Scott, what else could happen?

Daniel and Maria looked at her in confusion, probably not realizing why she needed the thermometer. Tennyson on the other hand, looked away, reminding her of Jasper when caught sleeping on the furniture.

"Have you seen it, Tennyson?"

He pulled it slowly out of his pocket. No wonder he could figure out the temp conversion so fast. Instead of being upset, his ingenuity impressed her.

"Did I ever tell you that you have excellent critical thinking skills?"

He shook his head slowly and held out the thermometer. Donna shook it, hoping to bring the temperature down and then ran it through water to clean it before using it on the wine.

She poured it into an elegant tulip glass with a short stem. The thick liquid measured an amazing 57 degrees. "If we hurry, we can get it to her before it gets warmer." She glanced around hopefully only to see the three of them looking away.

"Cowards." She placed a paper doily on a small tray and placed the glass on it. She carried the tray on her fingertips reminiscent of a train waiter she'd spotted on a family vacation. He told her his fingers could counterbalance the motion of the locomotive. With any luck, she could counteract the venomousness of the woman. Too bad she had no clue how to do that.

The Painted Lady Inn Mysteries

Book One

Murder Mansion

By M. K. Scott

A YOUNG OFFICER tied yellow crime scene tape to the rusty metal railing leading up to the porch. Donna's eyes narrowed as she considered the leaning rickety handrail. Definitely would have to go. Not only an eyesore, but also a legal liability if someone should stumble, grab the railing, which could snap off and send the would-be customer hurtling to the hard cement. Not good. *Mental note to self*: Remove the liability suit waiting to happen. Whenever a banister wasn't present, she made an effort to be more careful. With any luck, others would do so too.

A few of her new neighbors stood bundled up in coats with their pajama legs and slippers peeking out the bottom. The weather was nippier than usual for Legacy, especially since the small city straddled the border between North and South Carolina.

The other residents probably hid behind lace curtains watching the scene unfold, unwilling to chance the brisk winter morning air or the possibility of looking rude. Politeness served as a prerequisite in the restored Victorian neighborhood often masking people's true intentions. It was the reason she had jumped on the foreclosed home. It would be the perfect place for her dream bed and breakfast.

The front door swung open, drawing attention. A medic backed out of her front door, guiding a gurney. The second medic handled the back end. The series of steps leading away from the door made it difficult for the leading medic, a slender male. A couple of times, he lost his grip, bouncing the front end of the gurney down a few steps while the muscular woman on the back end chastised him.

"Come on, Barney. Grab the bar and lift. Give the man some dignity."

The residents bold enough to venture out in the morning chill leaned toward one another and whispered. She wouldn't be surprised if someone commented about the neighborhood going south. *Not good.* Time to establish her reputation and that of The Painted Lady Inn, before they both ended up with unsavory ones. *Suck it up, Donna.* Go do what you need to do. Damage control.

Her lips lifted in a parody of a smile as she crunched across the frosted lawn. An elderly woman glanced up at her husband and took a step back. Seriously, did she look that bad? Okay, no makeup and her father's old pea coat paired with a ball cap worked for her initial purpose of cataloging repairs, but was hardly appropriate for making a good first impression. Even still, the woman's reaction didn't make sense.

"Hello. I bet you're wondering what's going on." She held out her hand to the man since the woman's pinched mouth and panicked eyes didn't encourage neighborliness.

He hesitated for a brief second before taking her hand and giving a brief, firm shake. "Stan Whitaker. Yes, I did wonder what was happening. The sirens interrupted our breakfast."

Ah yes, a complaint. Somehow, she had ruined their breakfast. Finding a dead man in her newly purchased home put her off her cereal too, especially considering there wasn't one there yesterday when she did the walk through with the real estate agent. "Um, sorry about that. I came over early to start on the renovations."

The man's bushy eyebrows lifted with the word *renovation*. Yeah, she knew the type. They didn't think a woman could do anything besides cook and clean. *Forever single*, she had termed herself after being left at the altar at twenty-two. Telling people that she wasn't getting married after her fiancé found someone he liked better was one of the hardest moments in her life. However, it gave her the opportunity to do many things most would consider man's work, including renovating a neglected Victorian. Ignoring his attitude, she plowed on. "I wanted to get a rough feel for what I need to do first."

She nodded her head while considering ripping out walls as opposed to holding up paint chips and looking for mouse droppings. Her brother, Daniel, a construction supervisor, agreed to give his professional opinion and should be arriving any time now.

A car door slammed. "Hey, Donna!" Her sibling's voice cut across the chaos ensuing on her front lawn.

Her hand went up to acknowledge the greeting. She wished Daniel didn't have to yell everything, probably the natural result of working with power tools. "My brother," she explained, noticing the frightened woman had no trouble peering around her for a look at her brother. Donna rolled her eyes. *Geez, seriously.* The octogenarian was checking out her brother in front of her husband. The animated look on the woman's face demonstrated her brother's attractiveness. "I'm Donna, if you couldn't tell."

She forced out a little chuckle as if commenting on her brother calling her by name was humorous. It wasn't. Knowing any chance at meaningful conversation disappeared with Daniel's appearance, she spoke faster. Not only did the universe bless him with the wicked good looks of a fallen angel with blond hair and dark thick eyelashes all women envied, but also he had charisma. Women, men, children, even dogs loved him. As a sibling, it would be normal for her to hate him, but his constant concern for his older, single sister cancelled out the uncharitable emotion. Well, at least most of the time.

Her new neighbor stepped forward with an avid expression, earning a dark look from her husband. Ignoring the interplay, Donna spoke Yankee fast. "Anyhow, in the upstairs room, the attic really, thinking about making that into a parlor, great view, found the dead man."

A backward glance revealed her brother about two feet away and a man in a sports coat clutching a cell phone to his ear, strolling behind him. *Great.* Who could that be? Don't let it be the local news.

"How do you know he was dead?" The woman managed to tear her eyes away from Daniel's wide shoulders long enough to ask the question.

She inhaled deeply. *These people don't know me. Be patient. I need their goodwill.* "I'm a nurse. Have been for the last twenty-seven years."

The husband and wife looked at each other and smiled. The man met her eyes first. "A nurse would be handy as a neighbor. My Hilda has spells."

Oh great, another couple who expected free medical services, a common reaction when she announced her profession. At least it wasn't as bad as the men who announced they'd like to play doctor. That nonsense ended about the time she turned forty.

"Glad to help," she offered, not really meaning it, knowing she'd be saddled with a hypochondriac all hours of the day and night. *Give a little to get what you want* were her father's famous words about getting along with others, but it always seemed like she gave a great deal and got very little in return.

The scent of tobacco rode the air, causing her to pivot, searching the crowd for the offender. The man behind Daniel let out a puff of smoke as he returned her glance. At least he wasn't polluting her inn with his vile smoke. Since her window of opportunity would slam shut in about thirty seconds, she blurted, "I was wondering if you knew the man. Why he might be in my house?"

They shook their heads in unison, although the man replied, "Absentee owner. I heard he resided in another state. No one ever came around the last couple of years except for the real estate agent and the lawn service."

Lawn service. A possible lead, but there was little to do in the dead of winter. "Hey," Daniel called out, turning all attention on him as he usually did. Well, at least she'd had seven years of having her parents' sole attention before her baby brother showed up.

"Oh," she added, rushing her description. "Good-looking man with brown hair, expensive haircut. Preppy clothes, oxford shirt, khakis and windbreaker. Probably in his late thirties."

Odd that's all he had on in the dead of winter. Plenty of people drove from a heated garage to their destination with almost no braving of the elements.

Hilda looked away from Daniel briefly, her mouth partly open, ready to answer, when Stan did it for her. "Nope. Don't know anyone like that."

Daniel nodded to the couple giving them an easy smile that had them beaming back like recently picked sweepstakes winners. Presenting his hand, he shook both of theirs. Hilda had no trouble shaking his hand. Donna stepped back, realizing her time was done, but she needed her brother, who engaged in chatter about the weather.

Mr. Smoky eased up next to her. "I heard what you said about the dead man."

Her eyes cut to the man beside her. His skin, upon closer examination, appeared weathered and wrinkled, not at all the appearance of a reporter. Too old, too rough, not one of the pretty boys who ended up in front of the camera. His tweed coat sported wide lapels, indicating the man was no slave to fashion, or he was cheap, or possibly both.

Surreal. Everything had shifted at some point in time to left of normal. It could have happened while she slept. The man puffed away on his cigarette, getting the last drag before he dropped it and ground it underneath his loafer. Good thing they were standing in the neighbor's yard and not hers.

She tried for the world-weary voice of a sexy 1940s silver screen siren. "Yeah, what about it?" The scratchy tone of her coffee-less voice grated. Somewhere, between finding a deceased trespasser and calling the police, she'd put down her hazelnut coffee.

Her eyes remained on Daniel as he effortlessly charmed the older couple. Why couldn't she do that? It would be a useful skill for running a bed and breakfast, but her practical nature saw small talk as a waste. She had considered making her brother a partner, but his wife Maria quickly put the kibosh on that plan.

The man spoke, reminding him of her presence by her side. "You have a good eye. You remembered a great deal while only seeing the man briefly before you called the police."

Yeah. True, she tended to remember things. Was he complimenting her or accusing her? "When a dead stranger shows up in a newly purchased house, it makes a big impression."

"Understandable," the man agreed, patting down his jacket. Finding a box-like bulge, he pulled out his cigarettes. "Do you mind?"

"Yes."

Her quick answer stopped him in the middle of shaking out a new smoke. He pushed it back in with his index finger, replaced the pack and shrugged his shoulders. "Need to quit. Nasty habit."

Her top teeth rested on her bottom lip, keeping her from agreeing as much as she wanted to. She didn't know who the man was. It would be rude behavior anyhow. As an innkeeper, she'd have to learn to hold her tongue. Critical B and B owners probably earned very few return customers.

"Name's Mark Taber, detective."

"I'm Donna—" She never got to finish her introduction before the man finished it for her.

"Tollhouse, the owner, I know."

Her top teeth clamped down on her lip again. While she could use some lessons on the art of small talk and social etiquette, Detective Taber could benefit from an extensive four-year course. At one time, she played with the idea of naming the inn *The Tollhouse Inn*. Daniel discouraged her by pointing out most people didn't associate the words *Tollhouse* and cookies together. Besides, customers might believe there was a hidden charge if the word *toll* appeared in the name.

The detective reached back into his jacket, despite the significant look she gave him. His fingers withdrew a long narrow tablet instead of the dreaded smokes.

"Ms. Tollhouse, can you run me through your day?"

Naturally, he assumed she was single. Was it the man's coat she wore or the ball cap? Did he think she was playing for the other team? Then it hit her. *Oh yeah, Ms.* The outdated term identified women whose marital status was uncertain or those who bristled when asked. Hard to say which one applied to her.

She cleared her throat. "I left my coffee in the house. Could I go get it?" If she was going to recite her morning of feeding her dog, grabbing the paint chips and her short wait at Great Awakenings coffee shop, then she needed something to soothe her throat.

"No."

No, really? It was her coffee. She was the one who had overpaid for the meager paper cup of the sweetened brew she used to jumpstart her day. "Why?"

He furrowed his forehead, allowing his eyebrows to meet. Sure, he measured a few inches taller than she did, but definitely not a giant. If he thought to intimidate her, the man needed some work. She had the dubious privilege of working with numerous doctors who considered themselves gods, not to mention dozens of truly arrogant patients. Eyebrows in need of grooming did not do it.

"It's a crime scene." He said the words slowly, enunciating them as if she were either deaf or stupid.

Donna's nose crinkled in response to his condescending tone. "I know that. I called 911 when I found the dead trespasser." Someone might have considered her tone abrupt also. Her brother glanced at her, turning away from his enraptured audience and mouthed the words *watch it.*

"Trespasser?" The detective pushed his jacket aside and placed his hand on his hip, exposing his holstered weapon.

Was the move supposed to scare her? To prove he was a big bad cop who carried a gun? Somehow that made him better, smarter than her. Not happening. "That's what you call somebody who is on your property without permission. The fact he's dead just makes it more mysterious."

"Dead. Yeah, he's dead all right. Murdered."

Hilda gasped and grabbed her husband's arm at the detective's overloud words. The tiny woman directed a baleful glance Donna's way, acting like she had something to do with the dead man. Home values in the neighborhood immediately plummeted with Taber's pronouncement. Everyone looked at her, including her brother.

"Hey, I didn't know he was murdered." She held up her hands waist high, but dropped them when she realized it looked too much like she was surrendering. "I checked his pulse and called the police. There wasn't any blood that I could see."

"That's because…" The detective halted his words, noticing everyone's intent stares. "Never mind. Forget about it."

Taber stopped talking, aware he'd given out too many clues. Plenty of serious crime drama watching had her adding them up and unraveling mysteries was the one thing she could do better than her brother. For one, the murderer would know how he or she had killed the man.

Donna mentally retraced her steps through the house. She had opened the back door, plugged in the small radio she'd brought and tuned it to a top forty countdown. Not a recent one, but a prerecorded rerun of a previous countdown. The local oldies station played it every Sunday, one of the highlights of her weekend.

A small handheld recorder kept track of her comments as she moved through the house. Much more efficient than pen and paper. People tended to forget things when writing. Her coffee was in the other hand, the fragrant steam beckoning her, when she heard a sound.

At the time, the possibility of mice had her regretting she hadn't borrowed Daniel's cat, Miss Faversham, although the overweight, spoiled cat would be more likely to hide behind her when confronted with a rodent. She'd crept up the stairs, certain she would see the mother of all rats waiting for her at the top. No rodent was going to take up residence in her house. However, coffee and recorder didn't provide any suitable instrument to ward off a vicious rodent. At least she had on her pink steel-toed work boots. If she'd needed to, she could kick the dirty creature out the door, but she hoped it wouldn't come to that.

A creak of the wooden floor had the hairs on her neck standing, but as an inn owner, she'd have to be bold. Couldn't have vermin on the premises. An open door greeted her as she reached the landing. She *always* closed every door, an OCD quirk. Her brother often teased her by leaving doors standing wide open to see if she'd shut them. She *always* did. For a second, she suspected her brother had sweet-talked the real estate agent into going into the house and leaving a bunch of doors ajar, but that possibility disappeared when she entered the room. The body stretched out on the floor stopped her inner diatribe against the agent and her brother. Possibly a homeless squatter sleeping off a drunk? Plenty of vacant houses served as impromptu shelter for the opportunist. Another reason the bank had allowed such a low closing bid, that and she was the only person to bid on it.

Most people had looked at the peeling paint and leaning porch and envisioned dollars flying out the windows and up the crumbling chimneys. For one brief moment, her no-nonsense attitude fell away and she saw the realization of a dream. The building restored to its former grandeur with polished wood floors accented with floral oriental rugs. A tasteful mix of modern and antique furniture would create a welcoming atmosphere that would convey both luxury and coziness. Adorned in a fancy apron befitting a television cook, she'd serve a delicious gourmet breakfast to appreciative customers. She'd been perfecting her recipes for years. Usually the lucky recipients were herself and her co-workers, as she occasionally took muffins and pastries to work. Most assumed she picked them up on her way to work, even though she placed them on a crystal platter in the middle of the lounge table.

The man stretched out on her topmost floor stood between her and her vision. Panic overwhelmed her hard-earned calm perfected during a two-year stint in the emergency room that most beginning nurses endured before working their way up to the more coveted floors. Her current job, on the post-op floor, she'd eyed years ago thinking it would be a plum assignment until she acquired it. Whatever could go wrong after surgery from infections to cardiac arrest often did. Her phone sat useless in her purse two floors away. Unfortunately, she'd dealt with her share of dead bodies and recognized the signs mentally screaming, *No! Not here, not now.*

She'd inhaled deeply, realizing death was never part of anyone's plan. Maybe he was just sleeping. *Yes, that must be it.* The hand of fate that had grabbed hold of her secret fantasy of opening a bed and breakfast let up a bit. Sleeping vagrant, while not good, was something she could handle. She hadn't earned the unflattering nickname of Sergeant Abrupt for her gentle and soft manner. She'd placed her coffee and recorder on the wide windowsill.

The toe of her pink boot nudged him, not hard, just a gentle push, enough to get most people's attention, but not his. Her position allowed her to examine his clothes. Expensive name brands and a Rolex watch caught her eye. A number of the doctors sported similar watches. She had heard a co-worker mention that Rolexes could cost as much as a car or even a modest house down payment. Weird that such a man would stumble into her place for a nap. *Drunk. Great.* Still had to get him out. Kneeling, she'd shaken his shoulder, rolling his head side to side, but received no response.

Her index and middle fingers automatically measured his pulse while she looked at her watch. No pulse. Training had kicked in as she rolled him to his back and checked his airway. *Clear.* Her hands pushed down on his chest in a familiar CPR rhythm. She cursed her inability to call for help. Why had she decided to go into the house before Daniel arrived?

The pale white face and slack jaw told her what she already knew. The man was dead. She'd galloped down the stairs, taking three or four at a time, slipping once or twice. A grab for the banister had saved her from tumbling all the way down. She'd called 911 and her usual calmness she prided herself on had vanished.

"Dead man. Stranger. My house. Come quick." The operator made her repeat the address twice. The police came and ushered her out to the sidewalk while her purse, phone and keys had remained inside.

The moment she touched his wrist forced its way back into her mind. Even though she turned on the electricity for the home inspector, she hadn't cranked up the furnace. It wouldn't make sense trying to keep the uninhabited place warm. His skin wasn't cold to the touch, meaning he hadn't been dead long. Would they lift any fingerprints besides hers from the body?

The red and white ambulance moved away slowly. No reason to hurry since the man had expired almost two hours before, according to the medical examiner. The detective's voice broke into her mental review.

"I can see the wheels turning in your head. Care to share?"

"Glad to. Could we sit somewhere?" Far from glad, but lawyering up would make her appear guilty. Besides, innocent people didn't need lawyers, did they?

Author Notes

- ➤ If you enjoyed this book, please lend it to a friend.

- ➤ Write a review.

- ➤ Do you have an idea for a story or a character name? Love to hear it. I can be reached through my website at www.morgankwyatt.com

- ➤ Want to get free books, read excerpts before everyone else, receive special members only swag and giveaways? You need to be on the mailing list. Go over to my website and sign up. (I don't sell my mailing list and guard it as well as I do my chocolate.)

- ➤ Do you like humor with your suspense? Check out **Suspicious Circumstances: He Love Me Not.**

- ➤ Love to meet you, check out my personal appearances on the website too.

- ➤ Can you do one more thing? Go out and have an amazing day.

M. K. Scott

Made in the USA
San Bernardino, CA
05 May 2020

70609393R00132